Sivan

M-Gang Chronicles: Book Two

———————————

Robert Linus Koehl

Sivan (M-Gang Chronicles: Book Two)

Copyright © 2014 Robert Linus Koehl

Edited by Roslyn Gonzalez and Judy Koehl

Published by Robert Koehl – Dallas TX, USA

ISBN: 098578332X
ISBN 13: 978-0-9857833-2-7 (Robert\Koehl UNITED STATES)

PREFACE

This is a sequel. Though it should go without saying, if you haven't read the book, Zippy – M-Gang Chronicles: Book One, then you should probably go read that novel first.

If you HAVE read Zippy, welcome back.

I was ready to write this novel immediately after finishing Zippy. I already had the main parts of the story worked out in my head, and I was really excited about writing a few of the scenes. I just needed to connect a few of the dots in the plot and I'd have it.

More importantly, I really liked this story. So I was eager to write it back in 2011. But alas, life (and law school) got in the way and it took me a few years to put this one to paper. But it's been well worth the wait.

A major thank you to everyone who helped me edit, who taught me how to edit, and who generally encouraged me to write this novel. No man is an island. No author is either.

So enough with the damned preface. Here is Sivan, part two of the four-part "M-Gang Chronicles." You won't be disappointed.

TABLE OF CONTENTS

TABLE OF CONTENTS (CONT'D)

PROLOGUE 1 – AN UNTOLD STORY

Thursday, May 1, 1986

She heard a noise.

She was in the bathroom, changing clothes when she heard it – the sound of breaking glass. She had the morning off from school, but had to prepare for a night out with her parents, going to some fancy restaurant with her aba's co-workers. And she was going to be dressed for the occasion. Her little brother was playing in his bedroom. The babysitter hadn't arrived yet. But she didn't have to worry about such things any more. She was nine, now, and could go to fancy restaurants with her parents.

She'd spent the entire afternoon swimming in their back yard. It was warm enough outside now. It would soon be summer, and she planned to spend every single day in the pool. It wasn't the same as swimming on the beach in Haifa, but a private pool was one of the many perks of her new residence in Texas. It was certainly better than the cold New York dump they'd lived in for a few years after coming to this country. And the people here were nicer than in New York. They didn't care that she was a foreigner. But they did look at her strangely when she'd call her parents "imeh" and "aba" instead of "mom" and "dad." She didn't mind the strange looks, though.

1

The TV was on in the living room. The opening fanfare for the Channel 8 News was blaring throughout the house ". . . the spirit of Texas on eight . . ." For a moment, she thought maybe her aba had broken a glass in the kitchen, but this shattering glass sound was far too loud for that. She looked out of the bathroom door, and saw a brick in the middle of the living room. That's when she heard the voices. They were speaking in Arabic . . . at least she thought it was Arabic. She couldn't be sure.

Fear exploded down in her tummy. It felt like an electric wire shot through her arms and legs. Her parents had told her a thousand times: if anyone finds us, leave the house and run. Run as fast as you can. Find a safe place and call the special number, then don't go with anyone unless they know the secret phrase. Wasn't much of a secret, though. She was supposed to say "Mah Tovu." Anyone who responded "Oh HaLecha Yakov" was safe. Go with them. The problem was that anyone who'd ever been inside a synagogue knew those words. That song was part of the regular Shabbat service. She'd heard it every single week of her life. What's the use of a secret phrase that EVERYONE knows?

She heard her aba screaming at the top of his lungs as he ran down the hallway towards the bad guys. She bolted the other way, towards her little brother's room. She slapped her hand across his mouth to keep him from crying out, swooping him up with one motion. He was terrified. So was she.

She forced the window open, pushed him out, and followed as quickly as she could. Her aba's screaming suddenly stopped, and it sounded like a fight was going on in the living room. Her little brother ran—as fast as he could away from the house. She stopped in the front yard, right in front of the living room window. The bad men had just knocked her aba to the floor.

She stood there, frozen. She wanted to run in and stop those bad men. But she also wanted to run away. Her little brother had already run halfway down the street. Her aba was trying to get back up to his feet, but only made it up to his knees before one of the men hit him again. She was terrified.

For just one moment, her aba turned his head towards the

2

window, and looked straight at her. Their eyes locked. She saw one of the bad men pointing a small pistol directly at the side of his head. He couldn't keep fighting. They'd kill him if he did.

He looked terrified, but not for himself. It was for her. For just a second, she considered going back into the house and trying to get to one of her imeh's guns. Then her aba suddenly shouted at the top of his lungs, "NO, SIVAN!!! RUN!!! RUN-"

BANG!!!

The side of his face exploded. His body flopped to the floor like a rag doll—his arm landing and spasming for a few seconds out over his head. It was a horrible, unnatural way to fall. In one moment, her aba was gone forever.

BANG!!! BANG!!!

Stop shooting him. She wanted to shout the words, but her voice just wouldn't work.

BANG!! BANG!! BANG!!

The horror of what they were doing to her aba's body overcame her and she screamed. The bad men saw her. She ran. She ran with everything she had. She ran even as her legs felt like they were giving out and the burning in her tummy made her sick. She ran, even though she was crying uncontrollably. She kept waiting for the sound of more bangs, or the feeling of a hand grabbing her from behind. But these never came. She just kept running. She got to the safe place. Her brother beat her there by about 15 seconds. She made the call. Minutes later, grownups from the "Moss-Sod" showed up and took her and her brother to their imeh. A week later, a young girl she'd never met would shoot all four of the bad men.

But to this day, part of Sivan Katzav has never stopped running.

PROLOGUE 2 – THE GIRL WITH THE UPSIDE-DOWN EYELASHES

Sunday, February 3, 1991, 3:00 a.m.

He sat, handcuffed to the wooden chair. It was too dark for him to see anything, but he knew that his face was swollen, and that his shirt was stained all the way down to the waist with his blood. This was no police interrogation room. He could see well enough to know that there were no windows, mirrors, or cameras anywhere in this room. And that's what interrogation rooms always had in the movies, right? There was always a two-way mirror so that cops could watch you confess from the other room. This was just a dark wooden room.

It was hard to breathe. Not only did this room reek of sawdust, but his nose was broken. And this wooden chair they'd cuffed him to was way too small for a bodybuilder such as him. How did this happen? How did those children overtake him? Who were these people? Was he going to die tonight? Would he ever see his wife again?

The door burst open without warning. Blinding light flooded the room and he winced for a few seconds before acclimating to it. A middle-eastern girl had walked in, dressed like an FBI agent. She

5

even had a badge of some sort pinned to her waist. But she couldn't have been a cop. She was just a kid!!! She couldn't have been a minute older than 14.

She sat down with no introduction. "Your name is Brandon Jacobs. Correct?"

It took him a moment to process the words. She knew his name. How did she know that? "Yes. Listen-"

"Oh, I'll do plenty of that. We're very good listeners here. But I'm only interested in hearing a few things, such as-"

"Listen. You don't want to get into any more trouble than you're already in. Please just let me go. I don't know who any of you are. I'll forget every-"

"You know one of us. That's enough. We do not allow people to live who know about us." She paused for a moment, "I'm really sorry about that."

Sheer terror filled his chest. They were going to murder him!!! All because he recognized that brat kid. He was going to die here!! He struggled hopelessly against the cuffs. "Please. I have a family."

She looked at him for a moment with eyes that looked both sad and tired. "Your nose is broken." She leaned forward as though to examine. He started to respond, when-

BAM!!!

She punched him directly in his already-broken nose so hard that his chair fell back and he banged his head against the wall behind him. Fresh blood splattered out of his face.

"I'm not here to listen to you beg!!! I'm here for answers. And if you don't answer quickly," she pulled a gun from behind her back and placed it on the table in front of him, "various parts of you will begin to explode." She reached across the table and grabbed his shirt, pulling the chair upright again.

"Please, I'll tell you anything. I'll tell you-"

"Where is Stanley Benson?"

He blinked. The look on his face showed absolute bewilderment. "I don't know who-"

SMACK!!! She slapped him across the face so hard he probably got whiplash from his head spinning sideways. He'd bitten his tongue so hard that it was bleeding. And her hand had been drawn into a claw so that her fingernails ripped the skin on impact. He was bleeding again.

"I'll ask again. Where is Stanley Benson?"

"I DON'T KNOW ANY STANLEY BENS-"

SMACK!!! "Who is your contact, then?"

"I don't know what you're talking abou-"

SMACK!!! He had been in fights before. He was the wrestling champion back in college, and had taken a few stabs at boxing. But she was hitting so hard that it shocked him. She hit harder than professional boxers. How was that possible? She was just a kid. He realized that for the first time since childhood, he was in more pain than he could stand.

"I'll ask again, WHO is your contact???"

"I don't know anything about a contac-"

SMACK!!! SMACK!!! SMACK!!! She kept hitting the exact same spot on his face. The pain overtook him. "I swear I don't know what you're talking about. Please, just stop!!! I don't know who you are. I don't know what's going on here." He was beginning to openly sob.

"For a man who wants to live through the night, you don't know a lot. Do you?"

She let him sob for a few seconds then continued, "How do you know Mark Cohen?"

He took a second to process the question. "I'm a teacher. The Cohen kid is in my third period Bible class."

SMACK!!!

"If you lie to me-"

"ASK HIM!!! I'm Mr. Jacobs. I'm the Bible teacher at Collins Christian Academy. He's one of my kids."

She sat back again, stared at him, and sighed.

He continued, "I was out there tonight doing missions work. I have no idea what the Cohen kid was doing there. I was shocked when I saw him. I swear." Blood was trickling out of his mouth and oozing from his cheek. She'd probably loosened some of his teeth with the repeated smackings.

"Let me do the swearing, okay?" She leaned forward and put her hand on top of the gun. *"For four years, I watched my best friend stalk Mark Cohen. She had what you'd call . . . a trauma experience. She latched onto him, and watched him like a predator. Last year, she pounced."*

She sighed again, the anger building up behind her eyes, *"Last year, she took him in. She became his friend in one of his darkest hours. And she . . ."*

The young girl gritted her teeth, and started speaking at a whisper, *". . . I hated him for the longest time, but Mark Cohen was a good guy. Forget 'nice.' Forget 'charitable.' Forget 'moral' even. Mark was GOOD. He just had this inner goodness. And last year, I watched my best friend turn that goodness dark. She bled his goodness from him and turned him into a cold-blooded killer."*

His jaw dropped. He'd had so many shocks this evening that he didn't think anything could shock him now. But to hear this little girl describe the Cohen kid—sarcastic little brat though he may be—as a "cold-blooded killer," was more than he could handle. *"Listen-"*

She put her hand up to shush him, *"Last year, he shot an unarmed prisoner named 'Hassan' in cold blood. He even mocked the guy's religion when he did it. That's not the Mark Cohen I knew."*

She relaxed a bit, *"But at the same time, his OTHER actions last summer really made me reconsider my reasons for hating him—I can't hate someone like him for long. So as you can see, I'm a little upset about Mark."*

She looked Mr. Jacobs directly in the eyes. She looked utterly exhausted. *"Has Mark Cohen ever spoken of someone named Zippy to you or anyone at your school?"*

"Yeah. I've heard him mention that name."

She picked up the gun. *"Mark Cohen is very dear to me now. Over the past year, everyone who's ever cared about him, or pretended to, has betrayed him. And this evening, I watched-"*

She looked like she was about to explode. She cocked the gun, and shouted, *"I watched Zippy Dagan betray him!!! And I watched his five closest friends follow her!!!"*

She punched the gun right into his forehead, *"So while we're in the business of swearing, Mr. Jacobs, this is what I swear. I swear that I will MURDER the next person Mark trusts who turns on him!!! Is that you???"*

He started shaking uncontrollably, *"No. Please. I promise. I don't want to hurt-"*

"SHUT!!! UP!!! Your cowardice is pissing me off!!! I hate cowards!!! They make me want to kill!!! And you're a damned coward, aren't you?!?!?!" Her whole body tensed up. She was about to shoot him. He couldn't help it. He lost control of his bladder while letting out a horrific cry.

That seemed to be what she was looking for. She chuckled and her body relaxed a bit.

She moved in closer so that their noses almost touched, but the cold rim of the gun never left his forehead. *"If you EVER tell anyone about us . . . about what Mark really does, it will hurt him, and I will be very angry. I won't just kill you. I'll make you FEEL it. You understand, no?"*

"Ye- Yes."

"Good." Her demeanor changed immediately. She patted him on the cheek with her empty hand a few times, then sat back in her chair. She was still holding the gun. *"Some men from the U.S. National Security Agency will be here in a few minutes with some paperwork for you to sign. I strongly suggest you sign it."*

She leaned back, *"You've just joined an international counter-terrorism task force, code named 'M-Gang.' It's comprised of eight middle-schoolers. We are the proverbial sharp end of the blade. You stumbled onto one of our missions this evening. You understand?"*

He nodded. At this point he'd say anything. At this point, he'd believe anything.

"As it stands, two of our adult 'chaperones' have just resigned. They joined in with Zippy and her unfortunate betrayal of Mark, so I've given them a grand tour of the inside of an ambulance." She smiled, *"And even worse will be in store for you if you screw up. You understand, no?"* She punctuated her threat by pointing the gun back at his forehead.

He nodded again.

"We'll get a medic to patch you up. Sorry about the face, but your cover story is going to be that you got mugged." She smiled, "I had to make it believable. Anyway, you will not tell anyone about us—not even your wife, your mom, your mistress, your deepest confidant—NOBODY. Understand?"

He nodded again.

"We have everything set up: fake police reports, fake cops to interview you in front of your wife, and a really good story for you to memorize. Of course, this assumes you wish to continue living. Understand?"

He nodded again. She smiled, "then welcome to M-Gang, Chaperone Jacobs."

Then she got up and walked out, leaving him cuffed to the chair. Was this some sort of joke??? He sat there in a pool of his own pee for what seemed like an eternity. This was utter misery. He started to shake again. He couldn't stand one more second in this chair. It made his skin itch all over. He was panicking.

She walked back in with an adult. The adult un-cuffed him, and he stood bolt upright out of the chair. But his legs were weak and he stumbled forward onto the table. That's when it occurred to him . . . that's what was wrong with that little girl's face . . . her eyelashes were upside down, covering half her eyes. That's why she looked so droopy. That's why she looked tired.

He managed to get back to his feet and properly stand. That's when the adult introduced himself as Special Agent Sanders. The screaming, angry, ready-to-kill-him nightmare-child didn't introduce herself. She just stood there, staring at him like he was a piece of dirt she'd just scraped off her shoe. He figured her name would just have to be "The Girl with the Upside-Down Eyelashes."

Part One – Into the Setting Sun

CHAPTER ONE – YOU CAN NEVER GO HOME

Tuesday, September 4, 1990, 9:50 a.m.

What the holy hell has become of my life??? I don't even know where to begin. For the past week, I've been getting dressed-up into the most disgusting preppy nerd-wear in the long sad history of nerds. I've then gone off to Collins Christian Academy, where every single class—Math, History, Science, Bible, English—has begun with a prayer and a ton of church-talk about how you "get to heaven by faith and not works," whatever the hell that means. Actually, I think it means you can be as bad as you want, and it's okay, which is good for me because I've done some things that would frighten most people.

I'm sitting in Bible class right now. Let that one sink in for a minute—BIBLE class. Anyway, the teacher is a dead-ringer for Arnold Schwarzenegger. We call him Mr. Jacobs, although most of the adults like to be called "Brother" this or "Brother" that. He's a complete wall of muscle. He was writing something on the board when a little white spotlight suddenly appeared on the words he was writing. He didn't even turn around, "FROG!!!"

That was meant for "Ribbit the Frog" which is our nickname for this kid who sits in the back of the class. His name is Robert Jeffries, but made the critical 8th grade error of wearing a T-Shirt with giant purple frog on it during PE on the first day of class. I think it's the mascot from his parents' college or something. But it was enough to get him the nickname "Ribbit the Frog." He was putting his wristwatch up to the window so the sunlight would reflect onto the chalkboard and make this spotlight effect.

It was funny the first 10,000 times he did it. But that was last week. It was getting really old now.

Mr. Jacobs turned to the class. "So what was the Apostle Paul trying to tell us with this verse?"

I'm going to go insane. I'm going to go completely off the wall insane. I can barely stand one hour of Sunday-School per week, to say nothing of dealing with this stuff every day.

"Come on, kids. He's telling us that gossip is every bit as much a sin as all these other activities."

Finally, there's something I think I can agree with. I'm a walking testament to the dangers of gossip. Gossip literally ruined my life for a while. But for that story, we'll need to take a little journey back in time a few months . . .

Last spring, I was a seventh-grader at Anderson Middle School in Plano, TX. Yep, that Plano. Enough said, right? Anyway, a couple of kids started a rumor that I was gay, and a bunch of bad stuff happened as a result of that rumor. I got beat-up a lot, I got spit on, I got food thrown at me at lunch, and even worse things happened in the boy's locker room during P.E. class. All the adults in my life blamed me, saying that I brought it all on myself by being "weird" or whatever.

Then things really did get weird. A girl in my neighborhood named Zippy took me under her wing in the biggest way possible. You see, her parents are Mossad agents. If you don't know what Mossad is, just think "Israeli CIA" and you'll be pretty close, only instead of "spies," think "assassins." Then you'll have it.

"COHEN!!!" Busted!! He's caught me drifting off again. Mr. Jacobs may be young, but he demands your undivided attention. He won't even let you take notes in peace. "What are your thoughts on the matter?"

He'd been talking about a Bible verse on gossip, so I blurted out my best bluff, "Um . . . I . . I agree. Gossip is bad." The whole class chuckled. He let me get away with that much, and kept going on about the intricacies of Romans, chapter one. I don't know how I'm going to survive this class.

So this girl—her name is Tsipporah, but her friends all call her "Zippy"—introduced me to the M-Gang, and . . .

. . . oh boy, how do I explain this . . .

M-Gang is a group of eight kids, and I'm one of them. We're an international anti-terrorism assassination team, receiving orders from Mossad, and flying all over the world to catch or kill bad guys.

Seriously!!!

Last summer, we all flew over to Israel and went on live missions. In fact, just two weeks ago Zippy and I were in a big firefight at a café in Tel Aviv. We took out an entire team of bad-guys and I personally killed one of the most wanted terrorists in the world.

"COHEN!!!" I jumped a bit. Mr. Jacobs seemed less amused this time. "Do you think you can go for five whole seconds without drifting off into la-la land?"

I sat up straight and put on my best fake smile. "Absolutely."

So how do I go from getting beaten up by seventh-graders to being an under-aged James Bond? Well, Zippy is a master of several martial arts including Israeli Ninjitsu, also called Krav Maga. And she's been intensely training

15

me since last March. So is Zippy a ninja? I'd say "ask someone who's fought her" but they're all dead . . . okay, there are a few survivors, but they're all horribly maimed.

And my parents don't know ANY of this!!! They knew about the trouble I was having at Anderson Middle School with the rumors and getting beaten up and all. They know I'm involved in a "youth program" at the Dallas Jewish Community Center. They know I went on a "character building" trip to Israel last summer so that I could do "charity work," helping the poor and such. They also know that I picked up a few curious "sports" injuries, including a scar across my chest which my parents will NEVER know actually came from a super-hot-yet-evil terrorist chick named Adara, who tried to slash my throat and missed.

And that's the short version of how my life became a cross between The Karate Kid and G.I. Joe. So anyway, M-Gang is currently-

"COHEN!!!" I've got to get better at drifting off without getting caught. "Why don't you read the next verse for us?"

"Um . . . Romans 1:30 . . . right . . ." I started hurriedly flipping through the pages on my Bible. But just couldn't find "Romans" to save my life.

"Never mind, Cohen. Frog, take the next verse while Cohen plays catch up. And Cohen, I'm about this far from calling your parents."

I really hate this class.

So how did I end up here at this prep-school for Bible-thumpers? Well, my last school tried to do what Plano schools do best: sweep problems under the rug. They tried to blame me for everything that happened to me. So my parents took me out of Anderson and put me here: Collins Christian Academy.

So what's a kid with the last name "Cohen" doing at a Christian school? Shouldn't I be at D'var Adonai Jewish Academy with all my friends from M-Gang? That's an even longer story. The short version is my dad converted to Christianity and he has a problem with Judaism. The rest of his family is Jewish, and they have a problem with him, so they don't talk to us much. He only let me get involved with M-Gang . . . I mean . . . the Jewish Community Center Youth Outreach . . . because they promised him I'd get better grades.

You see, suburbanite parents are a religious bunch, just not in the traditional way. Their creed is "get my kid better grades." Their god is anything that will accomplish that goal. And they worship endlessly.

And this brings me to the last week and a half. What the hell?!?!?

I'm surrounded by goodie-goodies!!! I'm talking "Mr. Rogers Neighborhood" all day, every day. That's what it feels like being at this damned school. They talk about God and the Bible nonstop. And it's not just the teachers. The other kids are obsessed with "being good" and "knowing the Bible" and "soul saving" and I think I'm going to come completely unglued before this month is over!!! I was humming the tune to a Rolling Stones song to myself and some kid walked up to me and asked, "Do you approve of the moral message in that song?" Sheeeeeeesh!!! It's a SONG, people!!

I wonder what they'd think if they knew I killed someone two weeks ago . . .

. . . as soon as that thought went through my head, it happened: my hands started shaking. This was becoming a daily occurrence. But it usually didn't happen until P.E. class. Every afternoon when I'd go into the boy's locker room, my hands would start to shake, I'd feel uncontrollably scared, and I'd start brainstorming escape plans—where's the nearest exit, where are the sight-lines between here and the next room, etc. But now it was happening in class!!!

I couldn't breathe . . . there was only one exit in this room—the entry door—and there were only three people between me and the door who would have a chance of stopping me: Robbie Evers, Steve Forester, and Mr. Jacobs. I could burst forward and snap Robbie's neck before anyone would know I was moving . . . I could use a pen to stab Forester in the neck before he could react and get out of the chair . . . what would I do about Jacobs?

I was panicking!!! WHY?!?!?! I clasped both hands under the desk as tightly as I could. I wanted to bolt towards the door. Jacobs had his back turned. I could be 15 paces down the hall before he could even get to the door to follow me, by then I could duck around the corner to get out of the line of fire . . .

What the hell was the matter with me??? Line of fire? Mr. Jacobs was an unarmed TEACHER. Why was I panicking like this? I just started reciting in my head "M-Gangers do not recognize weaknesses, we overcome them. M-Gangers do not recognize challenges, we overcome them. M-Gangers do not recognize opposition, we overcome it."

Zippy had warned me that weird things would start happening to me over the next few weeks. She said it was a result of having killed someone and having people try to kill you.

I really wished M-Gang activities would pick up again. I needed to talk to Zippy SO badly!!! She was the only person I knew who'd been through this.

Tuesday, September 4, 1990, 5:15 p.m.

As soon as I got home, I called Zippy's house. No answer. So I called Danny's. His mom answered, but he wasn't home yet. I called Rachael's. Same story. Out of desperation, I even called Sivan's house. Sivan was the single meanest and angriest person I'd ever known, and she hated my guts. But something was wrong and I needed to talk to an M-Ganger. No answer. Finally, I called the M-Gang office number at the Jewish Community Center. Zippy answered.

"JCC Youth Program."

I was stunned. What was Zippy doing at M-Gang headquarters? "Zipps!!! It's Mark, listen I've got-"

"Mark?" she interrupted, "you should no to be calling right now. We're on blackout." That meant that we weren't supposed to be working out, hanging out, or even speaking to each other. It was a two-week cooling off period after combat where we just try to relax and get all the violence out of our heads.

"Hi Zipps. Listen, I know we're on blackout for the next week and a half, but-"

"Mark, I can't talk right now. I'm studying the Torah."

"What??? On a Tuesday???? Zipps, this is important. I need to-"

"Mark!!! I'm just getting to the part in Exodus where the . . . Amelek . . . Amelekites attack the Israelites in the desert. You know I have trouble with that passage because of all the weird tribal names."

My face went numb. I felt like an electric wire had shot through my tummy and up into my throat. "Amelek" was our emergency code-word for a worst-case scenario. Zippy would only use it in a sentence like that if she were being held at gunpoint and unable to fight back.

I took a second to breathe, "Well . . . I know that passage pretty well. Would you like me to come over and help you study?"

"No. I'm no sure there's anything you could to do. Is pretty hopeless."

"Okay, I'll talk to you later."

She hung up without saying goodbye. What type of person would be able to take Zippy prisoner? This had to be a bad-guy above all other bad-guys. It took me a half-second to decide what to do.

"Mom . . . can you take me to M-Gang??? Zippy put together a study-group for tonight."

I thought my mother would put up an argument, but the word "study" always snapped her to attention. The idea of me working on schoolwork put a sprite in her step and a song in her heart. This time last year, my grades had been terrible. But M-Gang promised her and my dad an improvement in that area. They delivered. And my parents have gladly marched to whatever tune M-Gang wanted ever since.

Not that my parents had any IDEA what M-Gang really was.

I ran to my room, grabbed my Beretta and two extra magazine clips, hid them both in the secret holster on my back, and headed out to the garage.

The evening may have been about to suck for me. But I was going to make sure it sucked for someone else just as badly . . . if not worse. My mom jumped into the driver's seat. My sister got into the back seat. We headed out to Dallas. I had the radio blaring in an attempt to keep myself calm, and to keep my mother from realizing something was wrong.

When we got to the Jewish Community Center, something was definitely off. There were too many cars there for a Tuesday. I got my mom to drop me off at the curb and head on. My family had left me here so many times that they no longer worried about anything happening to me. They headed back to Plano.

Two guys were standing outside the front door wearing suits. When they saw me, they both started walking over rather quickly. These guys might as well have tattooed "secret agent" on their foreheads. I didn't know if they were FBI, CIA, NSA . . . or imposters. Zippy and I had killed several assassins from a secret Iranian organization called Savak last week, so we were both on guard for revenge attacks.

"Hey kid. Center's closed today. You need to turn around and go back to-"

Like hell!!! I threw my backpack at one of them, and launched into the other with a standard groin-kick. He lurched forward, and his face came right down into my punch. It wasn't a very strong punch, but it was enough to bloody his nose. I didn't waste any time. I boxed his ears, and he went down—not a moment too soon.

The other guy was right on top of me. My backpack didn't stall him much. He reached out both arms to grab me. I bolted towards him, launching my right thumb into his eye. I reached behind his head with my left hand and grabbed his hair to keep him from escaping the eye-gouge. I pushed my thumb as far and as hard into his eye-socket as I could. He panicked. I tried to throw a groin kick, but lost my balance. The guy twisted his entire body, throwing me off of him. I hit the ground pretty hard.

I immediately jumped back up, grabbed my Beretta, and cocked it in a single move, just like M-Gang had taught me. I aimed center-mass on him, but he fell to his knees, so I didn't shoot. I hadn't destroyed his eye, but I'd gotten my thumb pretty far in there. I ran over as fast as I could and kicked him right in the head. He went down.

I spun around and aimed my Beretta back at the first guy, then back at the second, then back at the first. Neither were getting up very quickly, so I ran. There might be more of them, and I was out in the open. Damn!!! What if there's a sniper? I bolted into the building as quickly as possible.

Wow. I'd just taken out two bad-guys on my own. Zippy would be proud.

I hit the button for the elevators, then set the elevators to go down to the basement empty while I took the stairs. I hoped that if there were any more of these scary secret agent types (if that's really what they were), I could surprise them by avoiding the elevator. Theoretically they should be distracted by the empty elevator opening while I burst in from the stairwell and save the day. It was a good theory, anyway. I burst through the door with my gun cocked and ready . . .

. . . only to stare down the barrels of about a half dozen machine guns. It looked like a team of Special Forces Marines had paid us a visit.

"Drop it, Kid!!!" the leader shouted. No win scenario, I had to drop my gun. When six machine-gun yielding Marines have the drop on you, there's not much else to do. This evening was going to suck for me after all.

CHAPTER TWO- MR. OVERDRESSED

I slowly knelt to the floor, with my left hand up in a surrender position, and never breaking eye contact with the lead Marine. With my right, I placed the Beretta on the floor. Then I stood back up.

"On your knees, kid!!!"

I stood up and stared straight at the leader. My gut said that these Marines didn't want to kill me. If they wanted to do that, they'd have done it already. I decided to gamble that a little non-lethal defiance from me would not be enough for them to kill me. So I just stood there.

"I said on your knees!!!"

"Go screw yourself!!!" That seemed to make him shudder. I don't think he expected to see defiance in the face of five machine guns.

"I said get on your knees kid, NOW!!!"

I just stared at him, and in my calmest voice possible replied "and I said go screw yourself. Would you like me to write you some instructions on how?" If this guy actually was going to shoot me, I was at least going to die standing up. I didn't kill Shamil Hassan just to kneel down in front of my own killer.

The lead Marine looked like he was about to charge in and throw me to the floor. But before he could move, a voice rang out from behind him. "Dammit!!!! Another one?!?!?"

This overly-dressed guy in a business suit came running through the Marines.

"How did you get past the agents at the front door, kid???"

This guy looked way too old to be a spy. His balding forehead reflected the bright florescent lights hanging above him. He did look pissed though. He grabbed me by the shirt and slammed me up against the wall.

"How did you get past them???"

"I used the secret handshake." I smiled. I knew I was pissing this guy off. Maybe if he got angry enough he'd get careless and I could make a move.

But he didn't seem to get angrier at my sarcasm. Instead, he just sighed and turned towards the lead Marine, "Go get agents Thomas and Morris. They're obviously not doing much good up there."

I smiled, "You'd be better off calling them an ambulance."

He looked at me, absolutely disgusted. He shook his head and whispered to himself, "Not again." He dropped me and turned around to the Marines, "Would one of you guys please call the medic? Tell him to get back here again. Two more agents need a trip to the E.R."

The Marines all groaned and dispersed. The overly-dressed old guy pulled me into the M-Gang conference room. Zippy was sitting at the table, along with her parents. Sivan was there too. So was Sivan's brother Amir. Sivan's mom was standing in a corner. There was also my friend Danny Stein. But his face was all bloodied—someone had broken his nose.

The overly-dressed guy threw me against the table, "Sit!!" I looked back at Zippy. She nodded, so I sat down.

The guy started pacing the room, "So I know you passed a coded message to this one here. You must either be Mark or Aaron. Which is it?"

Well, no harm in him knowing my name. "I'm Mark Cohen. Who the hell are you?"

"I'll be asking the questions, son. You understand?"

"Then we're done talking."

"I don't think you realize how much trouble you and your little group are in. Now I know Ms. Dagan here sent you a coded message of some sort when you called. I want to know what it was."

There was no way in hell I was going to cooperate with this blowhard. All he would get out of me was name, rank, and serial number. Of course, we didn't have ranks or serial numbers in M-Gang, so I figured I'd substitute my team position and the order I'd been accepted into M-Gang.

"Mark Cohen. Team Aleph. Rank Beit. Serial number zero eight."

Zippy and Sivan chuckled simultaneously. I knew right away that they'd both given him similar answers.

"Alright, you want to play games, smartass. I'm not some backwoods terrorist like Hasan and I'm not going to get tunnel vision like Ms. Salimah. You can cooperate with me or I can show you what real trouble is."

I had no idea how he knew about Hasan and Salimah. A lot of bad guys knew about what we'd done. But so did a lot of good guys like Mossad and Shabak. But either of those groups would have identified themselves by now.

Mr. Overdressed started pacing the floor again, "Okay. You and your friends can sit here while we round up the others. And we will use considerable force in rounding them up. That is unless Ms. Dagan here decides to stop risking her friends' lives and possibly save us a few more hospital bills."

Zippy piped up, "You won't have too. Sheri, Rachael and Aaron were planning on stopping by this evening anyway." I knew what she was doing. None of the other kids' parents knew what M-Gang really was. If armed bad-guys suddenly appeared at their doorsteps, the whole operation could be blown. She was playing it safe.

He smiled and nodded, "Thank you, Ms. Dagan." He turned around to one of the Marines, "You, take Mrs. Katzav and Mr. and Mrs. Dagan to the next room." The Marine snapped to attention and the adults in our little circle all followed him out. The overly-dressed guy looked at the other Marines, "You four—you think you can stand guard over the kids till we get back?"

"Yes, sir!!!"

With that, he left the room and slammed the door behind him. I turned to Danny, "What happened to your face? Did one of-"

"NO TALKING!!!" Shouted the lead Marine.

I looked back at Zippy. She smirked the moment we made eye contact. We both looked over at Sivan. She shot glances back at each of us, and smirked.

Four armed Marines against one M-Gang unit? We'd just trained for this scenario last month in Tel Aviv. I turned around to the lead Marine, and in the meekest "Oliver Twist" sounding voice I could muster, I blurted out "Excuse me, sir . . ."

CHAPTER THREE – ENTER THE IDIOTS

Tuesday, September 4, 1990, 7:00 p.m.

When the door opened and Mr. Overdressed walked back in, the look on his face could have been the poster for a comedy film. I don't know what he expected to see, but it certainly wasn't four M-Gang kids pointing machine guns at him—the machine guns we'd taken from the unconscious Marines laying on the floor.

Zippy shouted at him, "Now YOU get on YOUR knees, Jackass!!"

"Stand down, Tsipporah." Her father's authoritative voice from behind Mr. Overdressed would have convinced anyone to put the gun down. So we all lowered our weapons very slowly.

Mr. Overdressed took a minute to compose himself. "Do I need to call another ambulance?"

Zippy snorted, "No. These guys are just to unconscious. We did no to make permanent injury on them."

He nodded his head, "Glad to hear it. Listen up. The rest of your team is here, and I want you to all hear this at once." He made a gesture behind him, and the other M-Gang kids all came through the door. "I'm Special Agent Sanders, National Security Agency. I'm the designated Agent in Charge of MYOP . . . or as you call it . . . M-Gang activities in the United States."

We all looked at each other, stunned.

"Sorry about the dramatic entrance, but we're still trying to figure out what's going on with this program. The previous NSA director green-lit the M-Gang program in December of '88. Then we got a new director in 89, and the program was ignored. Nobody on the American side has really taken an active role in M-Gang for at least 18 months. In fact, I was just read-in on the program last week, and-"

"So why are you messing with us now?" Leave it to Zippy to interrupt the guy.

"Well little lady, we were under the impression that it was still just an experimental training program. And it was supposed to be just that: training. Nobody thought any of you would be going live for at least five years. So you can imagine our shock last week when a couple of middle-schoolers from the Dallas suburbs took out Shamil Hassan and his best wet team."

Oops. I didn't mean to ruin it for everyone.

"Then of course, our embassy in Israel sends a message back to the State Department that the same middle-schoolers were the 'elite Israeli assassination team' that took out Adara Salimah. So to put it bluntly, you've managed to get our undivided attention."

Damn!! It!! To!! Hell!! My hands were starting to shake again.

"So we're here to put you guys to work. Mossad handed you off to Shin Beit, which I understand you kids know as "Shabak," last year. The agent in charge was this "Sarah Rabin" character, who I don't even have a file on. But the Israeli Consulate just confirmed that M-Gang is to be under the N.S.A.'s operational control for the next six months. And as the N.S.A. has designated me the Agent in Charge, I guess that means I'm in operational control of you kids. So I'll be coming up with a mission for you guys soon. I just don't have one prepped yet."

Zippy asked "So why have you contacted us? Why not wait until you have something you need us to do?"

"Good question, little lady. I'd like to get an idea of how you train and how you operate. That's the main reason. The other is that my superiors aren't exactly comfortable with a foreign intelligence agency having operational control of an assassination team in the US without at least a little oversight from us." He tried to smile at the end of his sentence, as though he'd just made the punch-line to an incredible joke that nobody got. It looked kinda sad. He continued, "To be quite honest, I'm not sure what to do with an assassination team that's authorized to work within the U.S. either. We usually try to take folks alive. But I'm sure we'll think of something. After all, we've had to move a lot of resources around over the last month because of this Iraq situation."

Yeah, they had the same problem in Israel. While we were there, Iraq invaded Kuwait and everyone around us started freaking out.

He turned around, "Mrs. Katzav, Mr. Dagan, Mrs. Dagan, could you three give us a few minutes." The three of them nodded and left the room, closing the door behind them. Sanders turned back to us and continued, "I'm heading back to Washington tomorrow morning. I'll return with a mission for you kids within two weeks. We've agreed that Tel Aviv will have no input into your operations while I'm in charge, so I'm going to ask you kids to keep all of your parents in the dark. Mrs. Katzav and the Dagans are active Mossad agents, and we want to see how well you can work with that umbilical cord severed."

Zippy protested immediately, "We never have operated

to completely alone. There always an adult."

"That's not entirely true, little lady. The file here says you and Mr. Cohen were completely alone and operating outside mission parameters when you took out Hasan and his team. And it says this 'Sarah Rabin' chick basically let you plan two of your own missions where she was little more than a spectator."

Zippy looked down and nodded.

"So really, you don't need an adult leader. You kids can handle yourselves. All you really need from an adult is someone to be there for show, and the occasional helping hand. And since I can't be here all the time, I've found two adults to play that role for you. I've decided to reassign a couple of local analysts to assist you kids. They have absolutely no field-training, and they know very little about what you're doing. But they do volunteer at a church summer camp for kids your age, so they're used to dealing with-"

"You're leaving us with a couple of untrained CAMP counselors???" Sivan interrupted.

Sanders thought for a minute, "Yes. Their official title is 'chaperone' and I expect you to cooperate with them so long as they don't intrude on anything mission-critical."

We all nodded. I didn't like the idea of a couple of untrained civilians intruding on our little group, but since the phrase "mission critical" is up for interpretation, I figured Zippy and Sivan could keep these two off our backs.

Sanders continued, "There's one more thing. Since you kids have all seen combat in one form or another in the last month, I'd like you to spend a few sessions with an N.S.A. post-combat psychiatrist."

"What?!?!?!" Zippy, Sivan, Amir, Aaron, Danny, Sheri, and I all shouted in unison. Rachael just dropped her jaw.

"Look, it's healthy. You've been in the mess with the bullets flying. It's good to talk it out with a post-combat psychiatric counselor. He can help you through the problems people normally experience after a violent encounter. Full-grown adults get nightmares, shaky hands, panic attacks. I can't imagine how it affects kids. And I'm not taking any risks. Besides, he used to work with Mossad, so you kids will probably trust him."

He looked over at Zippy and Sivan, "Just no telling your parents about him. We don't need Israel finding out we snagged one of their shrinks for our team."

It felt wrong. We had to keep the Dagans in the dark about M-Gang activities? I had to see a shrink and I couldn't tell my parents about it? It felt completely wrong, but we all agreed to go along with it.

Sanders continued, "So I'm going to leave you to meet your new chaperones now. By the way, the Dagans and Mrs. Katzav know about the chaperones, but that's about it. Nobody else can know this stuff. And I'll see you kids in about two weeks."

He turned around and left. No sooner was he gone than two other people walked through the door. They were two of the chubbiest people I'd ever seen at the Jewish Community Center. The guy looked like a comic-book nerd, complete with big-rimmed glasses. He also looked about 300 lbs. The girl was in her 30s, also way overweight, with the poofiest hair I'd seen. She looked like one of those cheesy televangelist wives. She flashed one of those toothy smiles that screams 'country goody-goody.'

"Mah name is Cheryl and this is Brice. Ah understand you kids are gonna be doin some special stuff, and it's our job to be your chaperones."

Oh sheesh.

"We're just gonna have so much fun together. We just have a few rules to get through first."

I wonder how long it takes for Zippy to snap this idiot's neck.

"First rule is this: there's pink and there's blue, but there is no purple."

Huh?

"There'll be no activities where boys and girls are left alone together without adult supervision. I know that you kids are just itching to experiment with sex-shuaaaal activiteeees."

THESE two idiots were N.S.A. analysts??? This did not bode well for the next six months.

Zippy responded immediately, "Then you two should be ready to give up your weekends because boys and girls spar with each other during our hand-to-hand combat practices."

Brice chuckled with a surprisingly high-pitched voice, "Not on my watch, kids. Boys don't hit girls, period. If they do, they answer to me."

Zippy got right in his face, "Then you can spar with me. What's the pressure rating on your best cup?"

He backed down, but his idiotic female counterpart continued rattling off a list of church-camp rules she actually expected us to follow. We didn't argue because it wasn't "mission critical" yet. We'd just let these two idiots pretend to be in charge for a while.

CHAPTER FOUR – YOU CAN ONLY RUN SO LONG

I woke up screaming and drenched in sweat again. Zippy had been right about the damned nightmares—they started almost immediately after we got back from Israel. And they weren't letting up. I had two major recurring nightmares. In one, I'd roll over in my bed to see Shamil Hassan standing outside my window, grinning with eyes like a gleeful child. He'd walk through my window like it wasn't there and grab me by the throat. None of my moves would work on him. I'd punch him in the throat, stab him in the eyes, kick his groin, try to pluck his hands off my throat . . . none of it would work. I'd usually wake up right as he choked me to death.

But that was the lesser of the two nightmares. The other was more disturbing. In the other nightmare, I had already died and come back somehow. I would be walking around my house, and my family was all mourning my loss. So I went into the kitchen and found an urn with my ashes in it. It made me FURIOUS, so I smashed it. While this seemed to horrify everyone around me, I figured "Hey,

they're MY ashes, I can do with them what I want."
Anyway, I wanted a burial at sea. Maybe this would drive
the point home. So I spoke to Elise and found out how I
died. I'd been knifed to death by a girl named Adara. Then
out of nowhere, there was Adara Salimah . . . but it wasn't
the same Adara Salimah who tried to kill me in Israel.
THAT Adara is someone I'd never forget. In the 5 seconds
I knew her, she kicked me in the balls so hard I both
vomited and passed out. She also tried to slit my throat.
She had grabbed me by the hair, and put the knife up to my
throat when her head exploded, courtesy of Zippy and her
trusty Walther P-88.

But the thing that sticks out most in my mind about my
real encounter with Adara (besides the feeling of my boy-
parts exploding up into my chest) is the absolute soulless
look in her black eyes, just before her head went ka-splat.
I'll never forget those eyes. Sometimes when I go to bed at
night I see those eyes as soon as I'm asleep.

Anyway, the Adara in my nightmare had those same
eyes, but was otherwise different. This one was my age - an
8th grader. She had the same knife, though, and she was
going to hurt my family. So I pulled out the tactical folding
knife Zippy had given me, and we started slashing away at
each other. While we were fighting, Adara kept talking to
me and pretending to be Zippy. But I kept hearing the real
Zippy somewhere behind me saying "Don't let her make
you hesitate AGAIN." The last time I hesitated against
Adara, I ended up sedated in bed with an ice pack between
my legs. And I'd been lucky. Not this time. This time I
didn't hesitate. This time, I stabbed this teen version of
Adara through her nose. As she fell, I turned to look at
Zippy . . . who had a bullet hole through her forehead . . .

Oh this new post-combat shrink was going to have fun
with those two. There were other nightmares, but those
were the two I remembered most vividly.

Thursday, September 20, 1990, 7:30 p.m.

I sat staring at the clock. All the magazines to read, all the shows on the television I could be watching, and all the trouble I could be getting myself into, and I was staring at the damned clock. My appointment was supposed to be at 7:00 sharp, but apparently the post-combat shrink's session with Zippy this afternoon went long. I couldn't imagine what all she told him. It was her THIRD session already. She started with him last week. Then they cancelled my first appointment so that she could take that slot as well. Then she took an extra hour this afternoon. Zippy's got some demons, but dang. Did it have to knock my first appointment back this far?

Speaking of Zippy, she was acting really weird during the last M-Gang training session. She tried to pull me aside early on. She said she wanted to talk to me about something critically important. But Cheryl saw us and started with her "pink, blue, but no purple" crap. Zippy said we'd talk about it later. But then she spent the rest of the training pretending I didn't exist. I tried calling her at home a few times since, but she kept saying to forget about it. Like I said, weird.

When the door finally opened, I found myself face to face with the shortest Israeli adult I'd ever met. The overhead light created a funny-shaped reflection on his balding forehead. "Mr. Cohen. Come on in. I'm Dr. Chaim Shadad. Please, do have a seat."

We shook hands and I went through the door. His office looked like a tornado had hit it. The chair was torn brown leather with tarnished gold buttons running down the side. I hated sitting down in it. And it was every bit as uncomfortable as it looked.

Once we got past the pleasantries, I began telling him my life's story. I told him all about the things that happened at Anderson Middle School last year, and he just sat there with a sad look on his face the entire time, occasionally interjecting "that's not your fault, son" . . . words I really wished more of the adults in my life believed.

Then I got to the part about Zippy and our adventures this past summer. He just sat there with an angry scowl on his face. Finally, I told him about the nightmares, the panic moments, and my shaky hands. That's when he started asking questions. "You've been describing normal combat fatigue. It's common in soldiers. It's not common in someone your age. But then again, it's also highly uncommon for someone your age to be in a live firefight. How do you feel about that?"

I didn't quite understand what he was asking. "How do I feel about what?"

He paused, "If Ms. Dagan had warned you about the nightmares, the panic attacks, and such BEFORE taking you to Israel, would you have gone on those missions with her?"

I didn't even think before answering, "Of course I would have."

He leaned back in his chair, "Would you indeed? Why?"

"I . . ." I couldn't think of an answer, so I just said the first thing that popped into my head, "because she's my friend. She was going to put herself in danger to protect others. She protected me. I owed her the same."

"You owed her your life?"

"Yeah."

"Why? Because she taught you how to fight off schoolyard bullies? That's hardly a life debt."

"She saved my life when Adara Salimah tried to kill me."

"That might mean something, but you'd have never been in danger if she hadn't gotten you onto the Adara mission to begin with."

"So what are you getting at? Are you pissed at Zippy for putting us in danger or something?"

He smiled, "No son, I'm trying to determine if you're

upset with her for putting you in needless danger. I just want you to be honest with yourself about your own feelings. It's okay to be upset with her. You have panic attacks now in the middle of your classes. You have nightmares. You didn't have those before she put you in danger."

"Look, you can stop right there, doc. Zippy is the only true friend I've got. She's the closest friend I've ever had. She stuck by me when nobody else would."

"You have no other friends in M-Gang?"

Dammit, was this guy a lawyer or something??? I responded "that's not what I meant."

"So tell me about someone else in M-Gang you're close to."

I thought for a second, "Danny Stein."

He looked back at my file on his desk, "Yes, the boy who went to school with you and did nothing when your classmates began hurting you. I imagine you're quite close. Anyone else?"

"Amir Katzav."

That seemed to surprise him, "Interesting. Doesn't his sister hate you?"

Now it was my turn to smile, "Sivan hates everybody, so I don't take it personally."

He leaned in, "Don't you think she hates you a bit more than she hates the others, especially given her life's story?"

I shook my head no, "I don't know anything about her life's story. I just know she hates everybody."

"Hmmm . . ." That seemed to truly throw him off, but only for a few seconds. "Well, I can't really go into her story—not right now anyway. But I'd be very surprised if she didn't hate you. I guess I'll leave it at that with Ms. Katzav. I'm still more interested in your relationship with Ms. Dagan. You're loyal to her, no?"

"Absolutely," I said with every ounce of conviction I had.

"And she's loyal to you?"

"Yes."

"She'd never cast you aside and take interest in another boy, would she?"

"I couldn't even imagine her doing that."

"But your files say that she took the same interest in another kid . . . Aaron Levin . . . and she distanced herself from him a bit after you came around. How do you think he felt about that?

I didn't like where this was going, "I'm not sure."

He nodded his head, looking like a teacher who's just caught you in a lie. "You know. Someone who ditches a friend for you will have no problem ditching you for someone else. You're a smart boy. You know all this. Does it scare you to think that Zippy might find another boy to take under her wing?"

I shook my head no. I refused to even think about this. "That wouldn't happen."

He sighed, "Aaron thought the same thing. But he hasn't given up hope, you know."

Huh? I think the shocked look on my face said it all. He continued, "Aaron still has what you'd call a 'crush' on Zippy. He admitted as much to me during his session yesterday. So you may yet find out what it's like to be ditched. Will you still feel as loyal to Ms. Dagan then?"

Alright, now I was pissed, "Hell yes. She taught me to fend for myself. She took away my fears. I'd follow her into hell. Why are you trying to get me upset with Zippy?"

"I'm not, son. I'm just trying to gauge your relationship with her. You say she took away your fears?"

"Yeah."

"Didn't she tell Ms. Rabin that exact same thing—that she'd taken your fears away?"

Damn!!! How did this guy know all this? I shook my head yes.

"And didn't she say she used that fact to 'buy' your

loyalty so that you'd always follow her when the chips were down?"

I reluctantly shook my head yes again.

"And didn't she say she was basically using you?"

"Yes, but she was just saying that. It was a ploy to get Mossad to keep me after the Adara mission."

He put his hands up as it to shush me, "Of course. But that didn't make you distrust her at all."

"It did for a while, but not since the Hassan mission. We talked about it. I'm not worried about it now. She's my friend."

He sat back, "Of course she is. And you're a loyal friend to her. I only hope she realizes how lucky she is to have friends as loyal as you. And I only hope she's as loyal to you in return."

I couldn't think of anything else to say except, "We're a team.

He smiled at that, then sighed and leaned in towards me. After a few seconds he spoke, "Look, teamwork is great and all, but in the end you've gotta take care of yourself. You're all you've got. Not M-Gang. Not Ms. Dagan. Not your nation. Not Israel. Nothing. Just you. And you have to draw a line between those things that build you up and those things that put you in danger. I want you to think about this between now and our session next week. Do you think it's healthy to put your life in danger for Ms. Dagan? Would you still put yourself at risk for her if she were to ditch you for the next guy, the way she did to Aaron . . . or even if she were to ditch you to give him the place in her life that you've occupied since last spring?"

I felt strange walking out of his office. Our session had only been 90 minutes long. But he got me thinking about things I'd rather not think about. Zippy and Aaron had been awfully close. They were friends long before she and I ever met. She started teaching him Krav Maga after some kids in his neighborhood beat him up, and that was at least a year before she started teaching me. When she beat up those kids in the mall last year, the first thing she did after getting home was to call Aaron about it.

I tried to shut that voice in my head up by reminding myself that Zippy picked me as the eighth M-Ganger, she upset her best friend Sivan by getting me into the group, and she and I went on several adventures last summer. But that just gave me something else to worry about: she saved ME from Adara, she saved ME from the bullies, she saved ME from the angry crowd of rock-throwing civvies . . . I still bagged Hassan though.

If Dr. Shadad was supposed to make me feel better, he failed miserably. I was still having nightmares. My hands still shook. I still had panic moments. And Shadad managed to add the unthinkable to my list of worries . . . what if Zippy decided to ditch me?

CHAPTER FIVE – THE INFERNO

Friday, September 28, 1990

Mr. Jacobs paced the front of the room for a good minute. "Cohen, how about you give it a try." He'd been going on for 20 minutes about the differences between the real devil and the "popular fiction" devil. This type of lecture was quite the norm for him. As always, he'd been babbling on about "Lucifer." I never quite understood why anyone called the devil that. "Lucifer" is a Latin word. It translates to "Morning Light." That doesn't sound too scary, right?

In Hebrew, the devil is always called "Satan" which means "enemy," or he's called "Beelzebub" which means "Lord of the Flies" or "Lord of Decay/Death." How you get from there to "morning light" is beyond me, although given the difficulty I've had dragging myself out of bed in the mornings lately, I'm not too inclined to argue with that particular word choice. Anyway, Mr. Jacobs had now asked me a question I actually could answer.

"Um, in the Bible, the devil followed a different syntax. He asked if God had really made a command, then he lied about the apple's actual effects, then he badmouthed God's intentions. In Dante's Inferno, the devil first drew an 'us against them' line in the sand, then he demonized God as some sort of tyrant, then he started laying deception on deception in his campaign to take mankind from God. So Dante's devil didn't start with deception. He just said 'me or him.' His direct lies about God were less subtle than the real devil's, and his other lies came afterwards, not before." I smiled. I was sure I'd nailed it. The rest of the class looked at me as if to say "huh?"

Mr. Jacobs looked at me for a moment with a tiny scowl creeping up in his eyebrows. "Not exactly, Cohen. But that's a very good catch. And that is what Dante's devil did. I was actually looking for something a bit more obvious. How about you, Frog?"

I quit paying attention at that point. I had more pressing things on my mind. Last night I had my second session with Shadad. He seemed convinced that I harbored some secret hatred for Zippy. He kept talking about how she exposed me to all this danger. He kept asking if I thought all the problems I'd been having since getting back from Israel were her fault. He also kept harping on this bit about Aaron.

I really wished I could trade in Shadad for another counselor. Part of me just wanted to grab him by the lapels of his cheap 70s business suit and scream, "LOOK, Zippy isn't the bad guy, dammit!!!"

But he's also made me paranoid about Zippy and Aaron. They partnered up for training last week, after poor Brice spent thirty-seconds in the ring trying to act as Zippy's sparring partner. It didn't work out to well for him, so he and Cheryl dropped their opposition to boys and girls sparring each other. They just wouldn't let us do any training without them there.

But Aaron and Zippy were together the entire day. I partnered with Danny. And I'm not quite sure I spoke more than five words to Zippy the whole time. In fact, I hadn't spoken to Zippy much at all since our meetings with Shadad started.

Something else had been bugging me. Last Wednesday, when Zippy arrived at M-Gang for our training session, she ran around and hugged every single one of the M-Gangers hello. But then she got to me, looked straight at me, and just walked right on by. That brought back the unwelcome feelings I had in Tel Aviv when I was worried that Zippy was using me.

Then she went the entire evening without speaking to me. It was like I wasn't even there.

Maybe I was just being paranoid. Zippy had a lot to deal with. She'd killed several people last summer. She'd come home to find herself under N.S.A. authority. She'd been dealing with the chaperones and their nonsensical rules. Yeah, I was being paranoid. I really hated Dr. Shadad for this.

Saturday, September 29, 1990, 9:15 a.m.

These Saturday trainings were completely wrong. It wasn't just that I hated getting up early on Saturdays. But it was weird that none of the Jewish kids seem to be going to their temples on Saturday mornings any more. Last year, they'd all been fanatical about being religious and going to temple. Now, we'd been doing weekend training for the past three weeks. And Sivan was the only one who'd put up any sort of protest over it.

I got to the JCC parking lot, and most of the M-Gangers were already there. Cheryl and Brice were lecturing Danny about something. Probably more of their idiotic "rules."

Zippy and Aaron were over in a corner, talking away. I suddenly felt a burning in my chest, followed by an extreme sadness. Was Shadad right?

I walked over to talk to them, but they seemed to ignore

me. So I finally just interrupted when Aaron was saying something. "Hey guys, when do we warm-up for today?"

Aaron seemed shocked, "Excuse me, Cohen. I was talking."

That pissed me off, "Well then you can just stop, can't you."

Zippy snapped, "Hey!!! Knock it off, Cohen." Since when has she called me by my last name?

I tried to play it cool, "Zipps, we need to warm up. It's after nine already and today is supposed to be-"

"Aaron and I already warmed up. You can go to warm-up by yourself. You are good at doing things by yourself, after all. Aren't you?"

I don't know if I was more shocked, puzzled, or hurt. "Zippy, what are you talking about-"

"Just . . . go warm up. I'm not talking to you about this right now."

What the hell crawled up her backside??? I went over to Amir, "Hey Katzav, you warmed up yet?"

"Not really. Partners?"

"Sure. Hey, what's up with Zippy?"

He shook his head, "I don't have a clue. She went and hung out with Sheri, Danny, and Aaron at Collin Creek Mall last night."

That burning in my chest became an explosion. "What?"

"Yeah. She invited me and Sivan to come along, but . . . you know . . ."

"She never called me."

His face squished up a bit like that confused him, "That's weird. Then again, Dagan's been off her rocker since you two got back from Israel." He pulled me close, "Hey, is it true you two made out on the flight, all the way from Tel Aviv to Dallas?"

Where the hell did he get that? "Uh . . . no. Zippy and I have never-"

"Well, the popular story around the gang is that you two got a little friendly on the flight."

"Her PARENTS were on that flight with us. Trust me Amir, nothing happened."

"Hmm . . . that's sad. Everyone else thinks you made it to second base with her."

I shook my head. Why did people compare this stuff to baseball? "I didn't even swing, Amir. There wasn't even a pitch to swing at."

After a few minutes, Zippy called the entire group together, "Okay, listen up to me. Today we do resistance to non-lethal weapons training." She opened her backpack and pulled out two mace cans. "These will not to kill you, but they can to incapacitate. And in live firefight, that is not much different because you will still to get killed. These can also be used to kidnap you."

Danny piped up, "Are those live?"

Zippy smirked, "Yes. There is no real defense against such weapons other than to shield to your face with your arms."

"So how are we supposed to defend-"

"You do not. You learn to fight after being sprayed. You learn to fight through the effects."

Oh joy. I knew exactly where this was going. It was going to suck.

Zippy continued, "So here is the drill for today. One of you will hold punching shield. One will hold kicking shield. Man in the middle will to stand over by wall. I will spray you in the face. You will to wait five seconds for all effects to start. Then you will throw two elbows to punching shield and two knees to kicking shield. Does everyone understand?"

Oh boy!!!

"After two knees, I will use water-hose to wash out on your eyes and face. You will have blisters like from sunburn on your skin."

I piped up, "Any suggestions or advice before we do this?"

Zippy's face turned hard, "Stay in the fight. Do what you must to do."

I couldn't let it go at that, "Shouldn't we practice without the real thing first?"

Zippy snorted, "It would make no difference. Cohen, we have decided that you will be first."

"Me?"

"Yes. You tough. You killed Hassan. You can do this, no?"

I grudgingly moved into position. Danny picked up the punching shield, but stood way far away. Amir picked up the kicking shield, and stood behind Danny. After watching Amir, I became aware that I was shivering—that's how scared I was. Zippy was about to mace me, and I was supposed to just stand there and let her.

I tried to delay by asking one more question, "Zippy, do you think that we-"

Her hand shot up and SPLAT . . . for a half-second, if felt like someone had splattered water across my face . . . for JUST a half-second.

Then the unbearable pain shot right through my entire head. My hands instinctively shot up to my eyes. I didn't want them to, but I couldn't help it. I tried to scream, but the burning sucked itself down through my throat and into my lungs. My legs buckled out from under me.

I heard Zippy shouting, "Get up!!! Come on, Cohen. Throw the elbow." I think I also heard Sheri and Rachael giggling. And Aaron was shouting some nonsense about not being a wuss.

The coughing was uncontrollable. My throat burned worse that the worst sore throat ever. My face burned worse than any sunburn ever had. But my eyes were the place where the truly horrific agony was. It wasn't just burning—it was stabbing. I started rolling around on the ground. I couldn't possibly get up. I couldn't scream for help. I was completely blind and unable to talk.

Finally, I heard Sivan say, "Hey Dagan, shouldn't you be giving him water now? He's not going to be able to finish the exercise."

Zippy responded, "Then he can sit there and burn."

"Dagan, what about the safety rule? If he can't function, you give him first aid immediate-"

"He can SIT there and burn, Katzav. Or he can to get himself up!"

Somehow that motivated me a bit. I tried to stand up. I tried to get back to my feet. But my legs just kept crumbling out from under me. And the pain just kept overtaking me. This was as bad as it had been in Adara Salimah's hotel room. But at least there, my body had the good sense to fall unconscious. No such luck here.

Finally, after a seeming eternity, Zippy came over with the water hose and started running it all over my face. It didn't do much good for my eyes, but it did soothe the burning on my skin. After about 10 minutes, I was able to completely open my eyes.

Brice finally asked, "Who's next?" But Cheryl would have none of it, "I don't think this is such a good idea for an exercise. Maybe we should call it quits for the day."

To my extreme and utter shock, Zippy agreed, "Yes. Cohen failed. No need to put anyone else on this misery. We will to it do some other Saturday when Sanders is here."

Nearly everyone else was in agreement. But Sivan stood bolt upright and announced, "No. I'm next."

Zippy argued, "Cheryl has spoken, Katzav. This is too dangerous."

"The hell it is. If Cohen can do this, I can do it. So someone pick up the damned shields."

Everyone stood there stunned.

Cheryl cleared her throat, "Miss Kat-Sav, I think it'd be best if you kids just hurry on up and take all your equipment inside."

Sivan didn't even look at her.

"Miss Kat-Sav, you look at me when I'm speaking to you."

Sivan kept her eyes firmly locked onto Zippy. Zippy just shook her head and said, "No Sivan. Is over." She threw the mace cans back into her backpack and started to zip it back up.

"Tsipporah Liraz Dagan, you will not do this!!!" shouted Sivan. And with that, you could hear all the air leave the parking lot as all six remaining M-Gangers gasped at Sivan's outright suicidal move. Nobody. Absolutely NOBODY ever uttered Zippy's middle name and lived. Even asking what the "L" stood for was a death sentence. But Sivan acted like nothing and continued with, "If you can do this to Cohen, you can do it to me. I will show everyone here how to pass this little test where Cohen failed."

"I know you can. But I am no willing to continue the training for today." Zippy picked up her backpack and walked towards the entrance. Cheryl walked over to Sivan and stated, "We'll talk about your defiance later Miss Kat-Sav."

The other M-Gangers followed Zippy and Cheryl, except for the Katzavs. Sivan and Amir both came over and knelt down right next to me. Sivan started, "Keep the water going, and get yourself some aspirins. In about a half hour you're going to get a splitting headache, and it's going to last all day."

"You've really . . . cough . . . done this . . . cough . . . cough." I wasn't going to be worth much as a communicator today.

Sivan smiled, "Yeah. Tsipporah blasted me last year, right after returning from Israel. Apparently Sarah did it to her. But I made it through all the punches and kicks." She gloated a bit at that.

"Cough . . then you've . . . cough . . . gotta be . . cough"

"Tougher than you?" She smiled, "Nah, just stubborn."

Saturday, September 29, 1990, 12:30 p.m.

Sivan was right about the headache. It was killer. Why the hell would Zippy do this to me? Especially when nobody else had to go through the training. She'd always protected me. Now she seemed to be the one causing me to get all banged up.

We all ate lunch in the conference room. It's not like we were using it for anything else. Agent Sanders still hadn't come up with a mission for us yet, so we were using our conference room for eating instead of planning.

Zippy got up at one point to make a phone call. So I used the opportunity to go talk to her. Aaron had otherwise been stuck to her like glue all morning, and all throughout lunch. As soon as she came back into the main lounge from making her call, I stopped her.

"Zippy, we need to talk."

"About what, Cohen?"

"Zippy . . . have I done something to upset you?"

She sighed, "I don't want to talk about that right now, Cohen?"

"Then when, Zippy?!?!" I wasn't used to talking this forcefully with her. And I think I was a little too loud when I said that. The other M-Gangers all went silent over in the conference room and started to trickle into the lounge.

"Cohen, you no to need me. You no need to talk to me. You do your best when you're alone."

That made no sense at all. "What are you talking about?"

"YOU. And the way you work alone. The way you do things alone."

That did it. I was going to confront her about what Amir had told me this morning. "Me doing things alone? How about you guys going to the mall last night? You guys didn't even think to invite me along? How can I help but be alone when you guys leave me out?"

She looked like she had back at the café in Tel Aviv when I asked her about a certain conversation between her and Sarah that I'd overheard. That little incident had led to a big misunderstanding between me and Zippy. But back then, she'd explained what was really going on. This time, she just hardened up and said, "Don't to be so sensitive, Cohen. I no am your babysitter. I no am your security blanket. And by the way, could you have been to any more rude to Aaron this morning?"

"Zippy, I don't think I was all that-"

She waived her hands and walked away. I blinked a few times. My skin was still pretty badly burned. I looked around at the others. Sheri and Rachael had these smirks on their face like they wanted to cheer for Zippy. Danny and Aaron looked like statues—no emotion at all. Sivan and Amir both had their jaws dropped.

Sivan shook her head in disgust as she turned to walk away. Amir grabbed her arm. She looked at his face and muttered "I told them this would happen. I told Imeh. I told the Dagans. I told Sarah Rabin. I told them dammit. Nobody listens."

CHAPTER SIX – HATRED'S LIFESPAN

Sunday, March 4, 1990

Zippy and Sivan had been sitting at the table for about ten minutes. Sivan still wasn't convinced, and Zippy had run out of things to say. Zippy wanted to bring "the boy" into the group, but she'd also promised that she'd get Sivan's blessings first. Now she'd gone and invited "the boy" to join—an idea Sivan just wasn't ready for. She didn't oppose the boy's entrance, but she didn't like the idea either.

He really wasn't M-Gang material, but Sivan was getting worn down. She'd trusted her old friend this long. And deep down, she wanted to protect him just as much as Zippy did. She just didn't think M-Gang was the way to do it. Something about how scared he was yesterday afternoon when they all went to go see him playing basketball in his parents' driveway just made Sivan pause. No boy their age should be that afraid. Nobody that ruled by fear would ever make a good agent. And she didn't really have much time left to figure out why she felt that way.

He was going to arrive within the hour.

The door opened. Zippy's parents and Sivan's imeh walked in.

"So, you've found the eighth member of your team, no?" belted

51

Mr. Dagan, like a mobster who didn't quite take you seriously.

A smile burst across Zippy's face, "Yep. He is perfect. I have to him watched for . . . a long long time. Here my report."

She handed a file to Mr. Dagan. He opened it, looked at the photograph and picture for a second, then darkness itself spilled across his face. He looked up and Zippy incredulously. "This boy? What do you know of this boy?"

Zippy shrugged, "I met to him at the cotillion dance classes when I was ten. He the boy I would always go to ride bicycles with on last summer." She left out the critical detail of watching him getting beaten up the day she'd killed that Iranian kidnap team. Sivan didn't say anything. She generally trusted Zippy, and would back her decisions no matter what.

But this was about to change.

Mr. Dagan handed the file to his wife, who looked just as surprised as he had been. She sighed and leaned towards her daughter. "Tsipporah . . . Sivan . . . there's something you girls need to know about this boy . . ."

Thursday, December 6, 1990, 8:00 p.m.

I walked out of Dr. Shadad's office feeling a little better. The last month has sucked like no other, and I'd always feel like I was going to get everything off my chest in my sessions with him. But I could only really tell him the basic facts: what happened. He seemed to have lost interest in how I felt about things. And he always managed to cut me off just before I could get around to the parts that were really bugging me. Odd for a shrink.

He also continued to probe whether I was feeling angry towards any other M-Ganger, particularly if they were Israeli and had the last name of Dagan. I'd started to suspect that Zippy was telling him things that were making him think she was getting sick of having me around. After all, Shadad had been right about her ditching me for Aaron. Zippy had all but ditched me in the last six weeks, and she had become extremely close with Aaron. She must have let this slip somehow in one of her sessions. Maybe Shadad was just trying to prepare me for when she did. Who knows?

As soon as I walked out into the waiting room, I noticed Sivan sitting over in the corner. She looked up at me, batted her upside-down eyelashes a few times, then got up out of her seat.

"Hey Cohen," she said with her usual delicacy.

"Hi Sivan. What are you doing here?"

"Amir had to change his session with Shadad to tonight. It's going to start in a few minutes. I have to . . . 'babysit' him for a few days." She looked disgusted, "My imeh's idea of punishment."

I laughed a bit. The idea of Sivan having to babysit the muscular giant was just comical. "Dang. What'd you do?"

She sighed, "I had a brushfire to put out. And my imeh disapproved of my methods."

The bathroom door opened and Amir walked out. He looked at me like he was ready to kill me. That was odd. Amir and I had always been close. What could he possibly be that upset with me over? He started to walk towards me when Shadad's door opened. "Ah, Mr. Katzav. Come on in." Shadad flashed that toothy smile which always made him look like that sleazy salesman on the first Die Hard movie.

When Amir walked past me, I noticed that he had a slight limp. That also seemed weird. Amir was always immune to pain. Something must be wrong with the guy. After the door closed, Sivan grabbed me by the arm and pulled me into a corner. We both sat down.

"Cohen, have you noticed anything out of the ordinary with M-Gang lately?"

Oh had I ever: the incident with the mace training back in September, the newly formed cliques, the way everyone had been acting—there was plenty of "out of the ordinary" to notice. Something was off, but I wasn't sure how much I could discuss this with Sivan. So I played it safe, and just said, "Well, Sanders is a lot different than-"

"That's not what I mean," she interrupted. "Have you noticed any of the people in OUR group acting weird?"

I hated this. I REALLY wanted to tell her. But I was afraid to tell her. She and Zippy were like sisters. Hell, the rest of us had started calling them "The Sabra Sisters" back in Israel. How could I tell Sivan, my arch-nemesis in M-Gang, that I was getting upset with Zippy, my closest friend in M-Gang? Unfortunately, in the two seconds it took for those thoughts to go through my head, Sivan saw it on my face. She sighed, "That's what I thought."

Yep. And that's when it just started coming out of my mouth, "It started with the mace training. Zippy just acted like she enjoyed spraying me and making me wait for her to get around to bringing me the water. And all the other M-Gangers acted like I was being a wuss. It's a damned weapon for crying out-"

"Yes, I know. Mark, I felt terrible about that. I wanted to go help you, but I was following Tsipporah's lead. And she'd always been so protective of you, I figured there was method to her madness."

"Yeah, well . . . that same day I found out that she and a couple of the other M-Gangers had gone to hang out at Collin Creek Mall the night before, and they didn't invite me to come along."

Sivan's face seemed to squish up a bit. "You know, they've been calling me and inviting me to come to the mall and hang out on Fridays, but they really ought to know better. A Jew does not go out on Friday nights unless it's to an evening Shabbat service. I'm always at home with my imeh lighting the Shabbat candles unless I have a Mitzvah to do. Like tomorrow night, for instance. My imeh and I are doing something tomorrow, but if we didn't, we'd be at home lighting the candles."

"Yeah, that's what I thought. But Zippy and the gang have been hanging out and leaving me out."

"Yeah, well if I'd known-"

"You'd have invited me?"

She hesitated, "It's not just Tzipporah. Have you and Amir gotten into a fight or something?"

That question took me by surprise. "No."

"Well . . . maybe it's nothing. I just thought-"

"He's one of the only M-Gangers I still hang with. Zippy and Aaron seem to have formed this little clique. Whenever we're at M-Gang headquarters, the two of them are always laughing, talking, playing around, play-fighting, and stuff. Whenever I go over and try to talk to them, they just turn away. They act like I'm not welcome. And you're right. It's not just them. Sheri, Rachael, and Danny won't have anything to do with me either. They talk about me like I'm not in the room, and when I try to say anything, they respond 'I wasn't talking to you, Cohen' or something like that."

Damn!!! That stupid lump in my throat was starting to form again.

Sivan looked at me like she understood. She put her hand on my shoulder, "Keep your head up, Cohen."

I shook my head, "And did you see that crap at Zippy's birthday party last month?"

She sighed, "Yeah. She and Aaron were being jerks. And honestly, I've gotten sick of the whole damned clique they've formed around themselves. You notice how they're so tight with Sheri these days? It's beginning to irritate me too. But hang in there. I've seen Tsipporah go through rough spots before. She'll come back around."

A bright light shined in the window. A car had just pulled into the parking lot. That was probably the "chaperones" coming to pick me up and take me back to M-Gang headquarters. Cheryl would have kittens if she knew that Sivan and I were in a room together, alone, and talking. As Cheryl was always announcing, "There is pink and there is blue. But there is no purple." Sheesh.

I looked down, "Well, Zippy told me not to bother showing up to the Hanukah party."

Sivan snorted, "She probably saved you a fortune by doing that. She likes to turn the dreidel into a hustle."

The look on my face must have given it away: I had no idea what she was talking about. So Sivan continued, "Sorry. I forget that you aren't Jewish. A dreidel is a little top with four sides. You spin it during Hanukah get-togethers. You're supposed to get a penny or pay a penny depending on how it falls." She smiled, "Tsipporah likes to up the stakes a bit. And she always walks away with a huge wad of everyone else's cash."

Yep, that sounded like Zippy alright. She'd done something similar on the flight to Israel last summer. I got up to walk towards the door.

Sivan stopped me. "Before you go . . . why don't you join me and my imeh for our little event tomorrow night? We need a boy, and Amir isn't going to be up for it. Would you like to come along with us?"

Hanging out with a fellow M-Ganger for the first time in six-weeks and actually having her want me to be there? Hell yeah!!! But . . . it was Sivan. Something had to be up her sleeve. Still . . . I had to take her up on this. "That'd be awesome!!! Where and when?"

She smiled, "We'll come to your house and pick you up around five. Sound good?"

"Sounds great. What are we going to do?"

Her smile turned mischievous, "You'll find out."

CHAPTER SEVEN – THE THORNE
SVELTES

Friday, December 7, 1990, 5:00 p.m.

Oh I found out alright. The little Katzav bullet-van pulled up in front of my house right at 5pm, just like clockwork. Mrs. Katzav insisted on coming inside and saying hello to everyone. She talked to my mom for a good half-hour while Sivan entertained Elise. I just sat around with my Walkman on, waiting for someone to say "let's go."

Finally, Sivan emerged from Elise's room . . . with bright neon-green fingernails. Ugh. She motioned for me to follow her out front, so I did. Once we were safely out front, Sivan leaned against the tree in my front yard.

"Tsipporah was supposed to be helping us out tonight, but she's off playing 'stupid teen hanging out at the mall' with Aaron and the rest of the damned clique," Sivan snorted, "so I used this excuse to get my mom to use you instead."

"Use?"

"Yep. We're teaching a 'girls self-defense' class, and you're the live dummy."

Oh joy!!! Sivan just volunteered me to get kicked in the cup about a thousand times. And there I thought she was being nice by inviting me to hang with her on a Friday night.

"Where are we going to be teaching this class?"

"Thorne High School in Plano," she responded. I was familiar with Thorne. That was the school I'd be attending next year if I were still at Anderson Middle School. Thorne was one of several "9th and 10th Grade" schools scattered throughout Plano. Each of these "9/10" schools fed into one of the two major "senior" high schools in the city. Thorne was also about a five minute drive from my house.

I asked the obvious question, "How did M-Gang get involved with Thorne High School?"

"We're not. My imeh is friends with Deborah Knight, who coaches the Thorne Sveltes. And I'm close friends with a few of the girls on that team."

The Thorne Sveltes were a dance team. That's a nice way of saying they were the hottest girls in the school. Girls who tried and failed to become Sveltes were relegated to being cheerleaders. Sveltes danced at all the sports games and put on shows of their own as well. And they were always dressed in skin-tight spandex suits which left nothing to the imagination regarding the bodies underneath.

After I went back into the house and got my equipment bag, the three of us piled into Mrs. Katzav's bullet-van. We arrived at Thorne right at 6pm. It looked like a prison. Thorne High School was a big white building behind a fire station in south Plano. Everything about it screamed "abandon hope all who enter here."

We went inside and made our way to the gym. Mrs. Katzav found the coach almost immediately and began talking about what she expected from the girls during tonight's training. Then she motioned for me to come over to her.

"And this is Mark Cohen. He's going to help me demonstrate tonight."

The coach looked at me unapprovingly. She detested having to allow a boy into a Sveltes practice. But I was "official" so she couldn't really do anything about it.

The 700 or so boys who attended this school would have sold their souls to be in this gym right now. Here I was, a mere 8th grader, about to interact with each of these girls—by invitation. I couldn't help feeling I should be enjoying this more than I was.

Mrs. Knight called the girls to attention, then introduced Mrs. Katzav. Mrs. Katzav spent a few moments telling the girls about basic self-defense principles, then introduced Sivan and me. We were her assistants for the evening.

And that was about the extent of my involvement for the first 15 minutes. Sivan and I stood off in the corner discussing our concerns about the new M-Gang leadership while Mrs. Katzav led the class in a physical warm-up. Then she led them through the usual BS about situational awareness and willingness to hit someone really hard. She had them partner up and start practicing basic punches and kicks.

Sivan and I walked around the room. There were about sixty girls there. Our job was to "correct" them whenever we saw them punching or kicking incorrectly. And oh did we have our work cut out for us!!! For dancers with "body awareness," they couldn't copy a basic front kick to save their lives. And they all kept trying to lean forward into their knee strikes.

Sivan pulled me aside at one point and said, "Oh, just let them hit. You'll never get perfection out of this bunch. It's more important that they just get used to striking with force."

"Yeah, I know. I just want them to stop siphoning all the power off their knee strikes."

"Yeah well, save your energy. The self-defense moves are coming up. You're about to take a beating."

I gave a resigned sigh, "I know."

"Look, if it gets to be too much for you at any point, just come get me. I've taught this class before."

"Really?" I didn't have any idea she'd done this before.

"Yeah." She looked around the room, "You know, statistically . . ."

She counted silently for a few seconds, ". . . 20 of these girls will be assaulted within the next three years."

She looked back at me. "If you can teach half of them to hit, hit hard, hit with conviction, and hit vulnerable places on their attackers' bodies enough times to stop them, you will have prevented ten rapes. So you see, you don't ALWAYS have to kill people to make the innocent safe."

After a short break, Mrs. Katzav called me up to the front of the room and asked me to choke her, for real. I knew what that meant, so I charged at her and grabbed her by the throat, doing my best to pick her up. And I screamed, "I'll friggen kill you, bitch!!!" at the top of my lungs. She did the standard pluck to yank my hands off her throat, with the simultaneous knee to the groin with rocketed me off the ground. Then she did the counter punch, right past my face, just like I expected. And then she disengaged, throwing a final groin kick which also lifted me off the ground.

Half the girls were giggling. There's something about people that they think it's funny when someone gets nailed in the groin. That's okay, we'd get that out of their systems in the first minute or two. The other half of the girls had gasped. They'd never seen strikes as hard as what Mrs. Katzav was doing to me.

We demonstrated again, three or four times. And each time Mrs. Katzav would lock up on me, I'd prepare to be pummeled with a zillion knee strikes, or for her to take me to the ground, or for her to position me for a neck-snap.

But she never did any of this. It was always just one or two groin kicks, then she'd disengage.

She had me reenact the whole thing with Sivan, step-by-step while she explained each move. And for good measure, she had me go all out against Sivan just once, so that the girls could see someone roughly their own age doing the moves. Then she had them all get up and start practicing the moves with each other, one step at a time. That's when I pulled Sivan aside for a quick discussion.

"You alright, Cohen? My imeh hits hard, no?"

"Yeah, but she's disengaging too quickly. She's not teaching them the finishing moves."

Sivan chuckled, "That's the difference between your training and what we're teaching these girls. They're not going into combat. They're not going up against terrorists. So there's no need to teach them how to snap a neck. They just need to do what we call 'stun and run' techniques. They short-circuit the attack, counterstrike, and get the hell out. There's no staying in the fight for these girls."

It was weird. This was a different type of fighting, but it made sense. The purpose was to escape, with an attacker who may or may not try to pursue. My training had all been focused on neutralizing an attacker who would definitely pursue to the death.

After that, the girls started practicing on each other. That's when Sivan and I started walking around and interjected ourselves among them, choking each girl at least once to make sure they could do the moves for real. They'd always be afraid to hit me . . . till the first time they'd actually hit me and not hurt me. Then they'd unleash.

After a while, Mrs. Katzav would interrupt and have me come up front for another technique. We did this a few times over. But all-in-all, she only taught them a handful of techniques. I thought it was completely inadequate, but Sivan assured me that it was better than anything these girls were going to get anywhere else.

It ended with a short speech from Mrs. Katzav on the principles of safety. Then it was over. Several of the girls headed for the locker room. Others formed into little groups. A couple of them wanted to come over to me and talk about my "martial arts" background, which was little more than a cover story.

After a minute or two, Sivan pulled me aside and introduced me to a tall girl with strawberry-blonde hair. "Mark, this is my friend Angela." We shook hands. "Angela is the Captain of the Thorne Sveltes. She also attends Temple Chai vey Chai-im." I recognized the name as Zippy and Sivan's synagogue in Dallas.

We talked for a few moments, then Angela had a question for us both, "So . . . this is kinda awkward. My boyfriend gets a little rough with me sometimes. He's not abusive, but I'd like to be able to fight him off."

I looked at Sivan, then looked back at Angela and asked her, "So what does he do?"

"He grabs my arm like you did to Sivan during the demonstration."

"Well, do what we taught you. Trust me. You can trust the moves. They'll work."

Angela just stared at me like she wanted to say something, but it made her too uncomfortable.

Sivan laughed, "I get it. I know what the problem is. This doesn't work without the counter-strikes, and you don't want to permanently destroy his manhood with your knee."

She rapidly shook her head yes. "That's it. Is there something else that will work without . . . you know . . . ruining his life?"

Sivan smirked, "Yeah, I've got a move. Mark, grab my arm."

I grabbed her arm, but hesitantly, pointing out that "I don't know whatever move you're about to do."

"That's okay, watch. I call this the 'boyfriend' shot."

She went through all the moves, and then locked up on my like she was about to murder me with a barrage of knees to the groin. "You see, it's all been the same up to this point. Now, drive your knee into him just like normal, only instead of the groin-"

She tapped her knee against my thigh—exactly halfway between my kneecap and my hip.

"Some people call this a 'dead leg' shot."

I was more than familiar with this strike. I'd been 'dead-legged' countless times at Anderson. The pain is unbearable.

"Shoot your knee into him as hard as you can—like you're trying to break his femur-bone. Don't worry, you won't break it. There's too much muscle in-between. What you're trying to do is turn every single cell in that muscle into bruise. You understand?"

Angela nodded.

"Here, try it on Mark."

I grabbed Angela's arm. She went through all the motions, then locked up on me—with Sivan instructing her every step of the way.

"Now, be careful. Mark is wearing a cup, so you can knee him in the groin as hard as possible. But he's wearing no padding at all on his thigh, so go easy on him."

BAM!!!

I tried to conceal the pain, and I'm sure she was trying to just barely hit me, but DAMN it hurt!! I put on my best "reassuring" face and told her "that's the spot." She apologized for hitting me too hard, but Sivan patted me on the back saying, "Don't apologize to Cohen. He's tough."

I tried to shake it off for a second.

Sivan continued, "I developed this move when my little brother Amir got big enough to fight me. I didn't want to hurt him. We both knew all the same Krav moves. So I needed something to keep him in line."

Then Sivan suddenly looked sad, "I even had to use this

move recently. Amir got rough with me. He tried to punch me. I engaged. I locked up on him and kneed his thigh as hard as possible. Three times. Rapid fire."

Angela looked eager, "Did it work."

"He cried for an hour. He limped for a day. My imeh was pissed. I told him that these were just warning shots. If he ever tried to hit me again, I would go for his balls." She looked Angela dead in the eye, "And that's how you should treat this move if you ever have to use it on a boy. Give him the most brutal dead-leg you can, and let it stand as a warning of how bad it's going to hurt if you launched that shot into his groin."

"And if he does get rough with me again?"

"Then you aim that shot into his balls and fire as hard as you can. If you sterilize him at that point, it's his own damned fault. You gave him fair warning. Now you show him where the fish pisses from."

"Show him what?"

"Show him where the fish pisses from. Make him understand what's what. Break his body! Don't just hit him. Keep hitting and don't stop hitting until he's unconscious. Break his spirit!! Don't stop when he panics. Don't stop when he begs. Don't even stop when he pukes. Keep hitting and make every shot a debilitating shot. Destroy him completely!!! He's brought this on himself and you owe it to yourself to show him no mercy. That's what I mean by showing him where the fish pisses from."

Sivan was harsh, but somehow I think Angela needed to hear that. Something about her struck me as being deeply fragile. She was cool and unreachable right now. But if she was into someone, or scared of someone, she'd shrivel up. That aggravated me a bit. I wanted to tell her that she should do Krav training at least three times a week for several months. But somehow I knew she'd never want to devote any more time to violence than she'd already done today. It just wasn't ever going to be her thing. And that was a tragedy.

We continued to talk for a while. I'd never thought of a dead-leg as a viable combat tactic, but Sivan was right. If you'd locked up on someone, and didn't really want to injure them, it was a useful alternative. It would cause a lot of pain, and it would hamper their mobility. But it wouldn't risk hospitalizing them like a groin shot.

Afterwards, Sivan, Angela, Mrs. Katzav, and a couple of the drill-team girls went out to dinner. And they brought me along. Being the only guy in this crowd was definitely NOT something to complain about. I completely forgot that Zippy and the M-Gang were off having fun without me. I completely forgot how left-out they'd begun to make me feel. THIS was an awesome evening.

Part Two – When Your Dream
Has Lost its Course

CHAPTER EIGHT – THE CONSOLE EIGHT

Monday, May 12, 1986

Little Sivan Katzav squirmed in the uncomfortable vinyl chair. This wretched room reminded her of the waiting rooms at the doctor's office. The chairs were all straight-backed. They were all made of torn vinyl. And she wanted to be anywhere but sitting down here. Where was imeh? She said she'd be right back. That was almost a half-hour ago.

The grownups called this place "The Console Eight" or something like that. They promised that this place was safe.

Safe. That word sounded comical these days.

If there's anything that the last week or so had taught her, it was that "safe" didn't exist. It was a lie that grownups told kids to keep them from being afraid.

Just over a week ago, she'd been "safe" at her new home in a little American city just north of Dallas. Now her aba was dead and she'd been bounced from house to house along with her imeh and brother for the past several days. And topping it all off yesterday morning, she woke up in this hell-hole called Houston. She hadn't been comfortable for one single moment since arriving. Outside, it was like being in a microwave oven. Inside, it was like being in a refrigerator. She was either freezing or burning to death. This place was terrible.

There was another little girl sitting across the room. She looked like a fellow Jew, one from the old country even. But you could never tell, especially in this place called Houston. There were a lot of people from Mexico in this city. Some of them were probably Sephardic Jews. But probably none of them were from the old country, even though many of them looked like they were.

Little Sivan kept looking at this girl across the room. Everything about this girl seemed wrong. The look on her face was that of an adult many years her senior. The virtual MOP on top of her head screamed that she hadn't combed her hair in . . . forever. Or maybe she just had a habit of sticking her fingers in electrical sockets or something. Either way, her hair was just a big disheveled mess sitting on top of a dark tan Israeli head. She was wearing Jams—these new outrageous shirt/shorts combinations which looked like an explosion of bright-neon paint splattered across an already blindingly bright outfit. She was swaying her legs back and forth. And of course she was wearing neon-blue jellies—plastic see-through shoes—as though her outfit wasn't ridiculous enough. She was reading a book entitled "History and Tactics of the Haganah Brigades – Overcoming Violence with Overwhelming Violence." That seemed a bit heavy for someone her age, but somehow it was the only thing about this girl that made sense.

At once, something about this girl also made Sivan uneasy. This girl was dangerous. Sivan didn't know how or why. But something about this girl screamed darkness. Sivan decided to break the ice and see if this girl really was an Israeli. She cleared her throat.

"Shalom. Aht Israelit?"

The girl looked up from her book, scanned Sivan up and down with her eyes, snorted as though she disapproved of EVERYTHING she'd seen, and went back to reading her book. "Ken," she said, as though she wanted to swat Sivan away like a fly.

But Sivan continued to press, "I'm Sivan."

The mop-haired fashion disaster replied "Good for you. I am not." She never even looked up from her book.

That response jolted Sivan. There's something really wrong with this girl. Nobody have ever been so rude to Sivan, ever. Undaunted, she tried one last time to make a conversation. "What is your name?"

"Why you to care?"

That did it. This girl had no manners whatsoever and someone needed to tell her about it. "You're rude!!!"

"Tragedy. Remind me to cry about it when I to decide I should care," she still didn't even look up.

"Maybe you should learn to speak English better, dress normally and comb your stupid hair."

With that, the girl threw down the book and exploded across the room in less time than it took Sivan to blink. She was immediately in Sivan's face. This girl was more muscly than most boys. She was scary. "What you say to me, you stinking swine?!?" she shouted.

Sivan recoiled in terror, curling up into a ball—almost entirely into the fetal position—in the chair. "No no!!! Please don't hurt me!!"

The girl snorted. "That not what you said, you cowering bitch!! Stand up!!!"

Sivan curled up even tighter, covering her face.

"Why you no stand up?!? You scared???" the scary girl barked.

"Ye- Yes!!!"

"Why? You no scared when you insult to my hair!! Why you scared now?"

"Because I don't want you to hurt me."

"So stop me!!!" yelled the scary girl, as she punched the wall above Sivan's head.

Sivan was still half curled up in her chair, "No!! Please!! Just don't hurt me!!"

"Stop me!!!" she yelled, shoving Sivan into the wall. "You think I just no hurt you because you beg?? I no care that you beg!!! You want to no hurt, you must to stop me!!! So stop me or I KILL you, swine!!!"

Sivan started crying.

The scary girl relaxed. "Is what I thought. You no can fight."

Sivan whimpered, "No. I've never been in a fight!!"

The scary girl sat down next to Sivan and put her arm around her. "Is okay. I no want to you to hurt. I Tsipporah. My name. I Israeli, like you." She smiled.

Sivan began to relax over a few painful seconds. She uncurled from the fetal position. It took a full minute for her breathing to slow down. Tsipporah was calmly comforting her and caressing her head the entire time. Sivan was still shivering though.

Tsipporah spoke at a near whisper, "I had to know. Would you just let me talk bad or make confront? You confront, even though you—how you say—shrivel after. So you brave. You just no trained."

"K- K- Ken. Ani lo-"

"English bevakhesha!!! We in America. I no can speak so good. I never learn if I keep talking Ivrit. You good at English. You help me, no?"

Sivan nervously confirmed with a rapid nod, "Y- Ye- Yes. I'll help you."

"You name Sivan. You the Katzav girl from Dallas?"

"Yes."

Tsipporah's face turned sad, "I so sorry to your aba. The same men come to my home."

Sivan hesitated before asking, "Did- Did they kill your aba too?"

Tsipporah looked down, "No. I only person home when they come. I shoot them with my imeh's gun." Her voice cracked like she was going to cry. "I make them to die. There was so much blood and . . ."

Sivan pulled close and hugged her. "Todah rabah!!!" They both started crying.

After a few moments, Tsipporah spoke back up, "My imeh told to me that I meet my new sister today—a girl named Katzav. My imeh say to me that you have NO training to fight. I no believe this when my Imeh say it. I can no to believe there is such thing as Israeli who can no to fight. But I fix this. No? I to teach you to fight. Then nobody to hurt you or family again."

Sivan took a second to process what her new friend had said, then *shook her head yes.*

Tsipporah sat back in the chair, "Then is good. I teach to you fight. You teach to me English. Two Sabras in Texas, no?"

Sivan chuckled. And with that, the Sabra sisters were born. Tsipporah L. Dagan began training one of the two people she would obsess over protecting for the next several years. Sivan never knew that she was an object of Tsipporah's obsession. But she would soon start hearing about the boy on the playground, nearly every day.

CHAPTER NINE – A NEW MISSION

Saturday, January 11, 1991, 6:00pm

The man in the picture looked pathetic. He was obviously short. He was mostly bald. And he had these round-lensed glasses on which made him look more nerdy than smart. And he had buck-teeth.

Sanders started the briefing, "This is our target. His name is Stanley Benson. He's wanted by the F.B.I. for operating a human trafficking ring."

This guy? This was the big bad guy that we were assigned to catch?

Sanders continued, "He kidnaps children and sells them as sex-slaves."

Aaron piped up "Why Cohen, he's just your kind of guy." Sheri and Rachael started giggling.

Sanders shot him a furious look, then continued, "Benson operates international smuggling pipelines. And they're not just for smuggling sex slaves. He smuggles children into slavery because he enjoys it. But he also smuggles money and weapons for terrorist organizations all over the world. He makes a lot of money and a lot of people die for it."

This was a REALLY bad guy.

"The mission is a simple one. You kids are going to take turns posing as runaways down in some of the seedier areas just south of Downtown Dallas. The plan is for one of Benson's kidnappers to try and lure you in. But since you kids are trained assassins, you'll actually be the predators and they'll be the prey." Sanders flashed that forced unnatural smile of his again.

Then he passed around another file full of photographs. "This guy is Andy Moore. At least that's the name on his birth certificate. He has more aliases than there are letters in an encyclopedia. So we've found it impossible to track him. We suspect that he's one of Benson's grab-guys. Our best intel puts him right here in Dallas. If we catch him, and we can get Benson's location out of him, maybe we can find Benson and put an end to all of his operations. Since Benson never does his own dirty-work, getting his grab-guy or someone else in his organization is the only way we can really go after him."

With that, Sanders took a step back like he was extremely proud of himself. He'd found us a mission to undertake. The chaperones were aghast. Suddenly, this whole "underage agents" thing became real for them. It was no longer a character-building youth-camp experience for them. It was real danger.

Zippy stepped up to the center of the room. "I've gone over the plans with Sivan. We're going to split into two teams, four people in each, just like last summer. We're going to operate out of a safe-house we've setup on the first floor of one of the skyscraper buildings in Downtown Dallas." She looked over at Sivan.

Sivan continued, "We are going to focus on eight city blocks which are known as havens for runaways. They're also known for prostitution. Each team will take four blocks."

Sivan started to pace as she continued, "Our four-person teams are going to be similar to our Tel Aviv missions. Each team will have an Aleph, Beit, Het, and Ayin. The Beit will be the critical person on each team. The Beit will shadow the Aleph as the Aleph walks around trying to lure Moore or whoever Benson's grab-guy in Dallas is."

She looked around at each of us, "Everyone is critical here. These guys are pros at taking out kids. We don't want to merely rely on our training, but we've also got to work this as a team. We have to overwhelm them with numbers. The Aleph's job is to get kidnapped. The Beit's job is to make sure the Aleph doesn't get kidnapped. Once Moore makes his move, both the Aleph and Beit are to use any and all force short of lethal to neutralize him. The Beit is responsible for the Aleph's safety. The Het as responsible for both the Aleph and the Beit. Whoever is in Het position will be on a rooftop in the center of the four city blocks, so that the Het can see what's going on with both of the ground agents. The Ayins will shadow the Het and coordinate between the ground team and the adults. If you need transportation or some sort of adult assistance, the Ayin will make the call."

Zippy piped up, "Does anyone have any questions so far?" Nobody responded.

Sivan continued, "Cohen, you're Aleph on my team. I'll be your Beit. Amir, you'll het. Sheri, you're Ayin."

Then it was Zippy's turn, "I'm Aleph on my team. Aaron, you are Beit. Rachael, Danny, you two can fight it out over who takes Ayin and Het. I trust to you both."

I felt a little sick at my stomach. Now Zippy would rather have Aaron backing her up than me. I saved her life last summer. What had Aaron ever done for her? It didn't surprise me though. All last summer I'd been looking forward to the Christmas holidays with Zippy. I was imagining what Hanukah parties would be like. I was imagining her coming to one of my family's Christmas parties. I was imagining a New Year's party . . . and maybe even kissing her under a mistletoe. But the reality was that I spent no time at all with her. She and Aaron were all but an item now. I was the unwelcome guest in her life. And now she wanted nothing to do with me.

At least I was on a team with Sivan. How weird was it for me to say that??? I was actually happy to be teamed with Sivan!!! I wouldn't tell Shadad about this. I was done giving him details. Every time I'd walk out of his office, I'd be so mad I'd want to go get in Zippy's face and tell her just what I thought.

I didn't notice at first, but Cheryl started having a meltdown. "Okay, this isn't funny anymore. We're sending these CHILDREN out to get kidnapped by real live traffickers RIGHT HERE IN DALLAS. We need to call the police. We need to tell the police what's going on." Brice tried to calm her down, but she was having a fit, "NO. This is crazy. We can't go along with this. Does anyone else see how crazy this is?" Brice dragged her out of the room. Sanders followed.

Sivan carried on with the briefing, "This mission is really going to suck. It's 30 degrees outside, and we're going to be doing most of our work at nighttime. It's going to be hardest on the Alephs. You'll have to dress like real runaways. You won't be able to wear heavy coats, thermals, or anything a sane person would wear in this weather."

Oh joy!!!

She continued, "But we don't want anyone getting sick, so each team will only go out for a few hours at a time. We'll get the Alephs back to the safe-house and let them warm up for at least an hour before having to go back out. The adults will be in cars waiting to come get us."

The door opened, Sanders and the chaperones came back in. Apparently they'd managed to calm Cheryl back down and get her back on track.

Zippy took back over after they got Cheryl seated, "My

team meets on Monday and Wednesday this week to train and do dry runs. Sivan's team on Tuesday and Thursday. Everyone who has sessions with Shadad, your sessions are already rescheduled to days when you no to train."

Sivan finished the meeting with, "Let's get this mission over with quickly. I don't like using my friends for bait, and I really don't like working in the cold."

We all nodded in agreement.

CHAPTER TEN – THE DARKNESS KNOWS

I was confused. A moment ago I'd been in the hallway between the lunch room and the gym at Collins Christian Academy. Now I was in the entry to the boys' locker room at Anderson Middle School in Plano. I looked over to where the weight room should be, and it was the hallway at my grandparents' house. My old classmate Dave was there, but he was wearing a girl's dress. It was a bright blue dress, with bright blue pumps, and black pantyhose.

I ran away from him, right into the boys' locker room. There I ran into a dozen of my former classmates from Anderson. They were all in gym cloths. One of them started punching me in the arm. The others were calling me names: "faggot," "queer," "homo," "cocksucker" etc. They were surrounding me. I looked back to the weight room. Dave was still wearing a dress, but he'd had taken off his pumps, and was jogging in place with a clownish smile on his face, the girls' hose he was wearing were starting to rip.

I was suddenly frightened. The kids in the locker

room had completely surrounded me and were hurting me. I grabbed for my Beretta, but it wasn't there. Didn't I know that I wasn't part of M-Gang yet when stuff like this still happened? M-Gang didn't come around till after the kids all hurt me in the locker room. Why didn't I remember that? I started punching, kicking, and biting my way through this crowd. I fought my way through them and bolted towards the door.

Zippy was standing in the door. Her upper lip curled up in disgust as she looked at me. She shook her head, then she looked at the kids behind me and said "take him." The other kids all jumped on me at once. I tried to fight but there were too many of them and they were all too strong.

The last thing I remember before I woke up screaming was Zippy saying, "You'll never be Aaron, Mark. You'll always be the school faggot."

Saturday, February 2, 1991, sometime between 8 pm and midnight.

This!!!
Mission!!!
Sucked!!!

I'd spent the last couple of Saturday nights in the freezing cold, without enough clothes on to keep me warm. Every week has been the same routine. I'd go out at eight, walk around these horrific seedy neighborhoods for two hours, then return to the safehouse. I'd go back out at 11 and do it for another two hours. I'd go back around 3, and do it until 5. Then I'd go home and get an hour's sleep before my parents would insist on me being up for church.

What's more, this mission disintegrated from the original plan. The "adult transportation" which was supposed to take us back to the safe house lasted all of one day. Then it became "get a cab" as though any cab would be caught dead in those neighborhoods. Then it became a long walk to a neighborhood where you COULD get a cab, as though there was one within 2 miles walk. Finally, it became bicycles. Yep, after patrolling for Moore or whoever Benson's grab-guy was for two hours, we had to BIKE back to the safe-house.

And all of this was in 30-degree weather. I was Aleph on this team, which meant that I was just wearing a tank-top with an open windbreaker.

This mission sucked!!!

I got to M-Gang headquarters this morning at 11am. Then I ate lunch by myself—not that I was the only one there, but nobody at M-Gang was speaking to me anymore. They all seemed to hate me, except for Sivan who had always merely tolerated my presence.

Then I spent all afternoon being invisible. I didn't know why I was even still a part of this group. They all hated me. Even Zippy. I didn't know why, but she'd grown to outright hate me.

I tried to talk to Shadad about it, but he'd just say that I needed to "be tough" and "know my friends from my enemies" and "protect my friends," and "rain hell on my enemies."

I just wished I could get my friends to remember that I was one of them.

This evening, we got a bit of good news, though. An anonymous tipper had called a government hotline to tell them that Moore was in Dallas this weekend. He was likely grabbing kids for Benson this weekend.

We all agreed to step up our efforts this evening: patrol longer and take shorter breaks, even though it was insanely cold outside this weekend. The Ayins were staying behind at the safe-house so that we could travel more quickly.

My first patrol this evening was three hours long. I walked around those four city blocks at least 20 times. Sivan shadowed me from about 50 ft. behind. Amir was on the rooftops. And we all had microphones with ear-coms just like in Tel Aviv. The coms just didn't buzz all that often because nobody really had all that much to say.

After 20 minutes, I was shivering uncontrollably. After an hour, I was delirious. I forgot where I was a few times. Sivan would occasionally buzz me on the coms to say "wake up, Cohen" then go silent again.

Around 10:45, we gave up on our first patrol, and headed for the bikes. I could barely even grip the handlebars because my hands were so badly frozen. Biking in this cold was its own version of hell because speed just made the wind bite you that much harder.

It took us a half hour, but we made our way back to the safe house where the Ayins had been sipping hot chocolate with the chaperones all evening waiting for us to return. We ditched the bikes out front. Sivan and Amir went in, but I had to make my way around back to avoid suspicion.

I went in through the back door. As soon as it closed, Sivan was there with a blanket. She threw it over me and ran me to the lobby. She ushered everyone else out of the way to a space heater. I huddled by it, still shivering uncontrollably. My skin was red. The space-heater felt like it was setting me ablaze. This mission really sucked. Did I mention that? I just looked at the floor. I was really desperate for this mission to be over.

After about ten minutes, the chaperones joined us to talk about our next steps. This evening was just getting better and better.

CHAPTER ELEVEN – A DISH BEST SERVED COLD

Brice put on his best "coaches" voice, "Cohen, you're back out there in 20-minutes."

I nodded, still looking down at the floor and huddling as close to the heater as I could. Were they trying to kill me? I knew that Benson's grab guy was probably still out there, but I'd been on the street since 8pm—three hours in the freezing cold wearing a tank-top and a paper-thin unbuttoned windbreaker. This was torture.

Danny seemed to get upset by Brice's enthusiasm, "Hey, we haven't eaten since noon. Could we take a break? I'm hungry!!!"

Several others chimed in their agreement. M-Gang missions had never been this short on food before. The chaperones seemed to be swayed. "Okay, we'll go to the pancake house over on Lemon. That's only about 10-minutes away, and they're open 24-hours."

Yes!!! I get a break. I can sit in a nice warm restaurant

Zippy stopped her, "Mark can't leave now. We have a good chance of catching Benson's grab guy this evening.

I'm sorry, but he can't join us."

I sighed. This hurt. Zippy was at it again—making sure I got left behind. This time I put up a fight. "I haven't eaten since noon. How am I supposed to fight off the grab guy if he-"

"You'll manage!!! You always do. In fact, you do your best work alone, don't you?" There was a hint of bitterness in her voice, and I honestly had no idea what that last bit meant. When had I ever gone off and tried to do something alone on a mission?

Sivan piped up, "Somebody's got to shadow him. Who's up?" She looked around. The boys were all looking at the floor, and the girls were all looking at the chaperones.

Brice finally answered, "He can handle himself for an hour. We'll get back and cover him."

Sivan shook her head, "We don't leave people out there alone."

"Oh, it's not like anything's going to happen while he's out there. We've been at this for weeks and nothing's happened."

Sivan smirked, "If that's true, then why not just bring him with us. If nothing's going to happen, then there's no reason Mark can't get a break and come eat with-"

"Sivan," Zippy walked towards her calmly, "it's just an hour. Mark can handle it. Can't you, Mark?" She looked back at me. I just looked at the ground.

Brice seemed triumphant, "It's settled then. Everyone else to the pancake house. Cohen, we'll touch base when we return."

I looked up for a second, "When you get back, do I get a dinner break?"

Brice hesitated, "We'll figure something out when we get back."

"And what do I do if I run into trouble?"

"Do your best to get back here and wait for us."

Sivan looked absolutely disgusted. "Fine. You all want

to treat this like some stupid game. I'll stay behind and watch Mark. Then he and I will rotate out and get dinner when you all get back."

"Ahem" Cheryl made a spectacle of clearing her throat, "I think you've forgotten our little rule Ms. Kat-Sav. There is blue and there is pink. There is no purple. Boys and girls are not to be left alone together. You think we're going to leave you two alone so you can be tempted into sex-shu-all situations?"

Sivan had finally had it. I thought she was going to shoot Cheryl dead on the spot. "Your rules, tourist, not mine."

"Excuse me?"

"I said 'YOUR RULES, NOT MINE' tourist. And I don't follow YOUR rules."

"Young lady, we need to come to a little understanding about something right now!"

"You're damned right we do!!! I'm a trained assassin. You're an ACTRESS!!! Your job is to PRETEND to be my 'adult chaperone' for situations where that will make my job easier. Other than that, you stay the hell out of my way. You are in charge of NOTHING. You do not give me orders. You don't even make suggestions."

Zippy tried to intervene and calm her down, but she shoved Zippy away. "NO!!! I've had enough of these . . . tourists."

Cheryl was outraged, "We'll discuss this when we get back to M-Gang, young lady."

"You better pray to God we don't." I'd never seen Sivan looking this serious before, and that's saying something. "Because if we do, I'm going to put you in an ambulance. Do you understand me? Trained assassin versus the actress—I don't think you want that conversation."

Sivan looked over at Zippy. "I put Mark in danger during our first mission in Tel Aviv. I left you and Mark behind during our last mission there. Never again." Those last two words seemed to jolt Zippy. Something about that Israeli motto seemed to create a locked bond between them at that moment.

At this point, Brice had walked over as though he had something to say, but Sivan cut him off, "And if either of you ACTORS want to TRY and interfere with my in-field decisions, step up now."

Brice and Cheryl both backed off.

"That's what I thought. So why don't you all just run along to the pancake house and leave the real work to me and Mark. I'll keep watch on him. You can all relax in the warm, and we'll do the real work."

About half the M-Gangers hesitated. So Sivan shouted "GO." Zippy and Amir hesitated the longest. They both looked at Sivan like they wanted to tell her something, but not in front of everyone else. So they all filed out of the room. The "chaperones" stayed behind for a second. So Sivan got another little word in, "If either of you ever try to isolate Mark or any member of my team again, you'll be maimed for life. I swear it!!! Now get the hell out of my sight before I make one of you bleed."

I think they both wanted to respond. But they both wisely just kept their mouths shut and walked out the door. I can't imagine what the conversation at the pancake house must have been like.

I started to put my "kidnap me" outfit back on, complete with my hidden gun holster. Sivan put her hand on my shoulder. "Don't worry, Cohen. I'm a great sniper. I will watch you from the rooftops. Nothing will hurt you on my watch." She leaned in so that we were nearly nose-to-nose, "nothing!!!" She meant it.

So we headed out again, and the dark back-alleys of south Dallas welcomed us, as did the horrid cold.

It wasn't two minutes before I was shivering. The coms crackled. "You still with me, Cohen."

"Y- Ye- Yes."

"Good. Just listen to my voice and keep talking. I'm going to get you through this."

I couldn't stand it. I zipped up the little wind-breaker jacket. I was supposed to leave it open to attract any possible sex predators, but it was just so damned cold.

Sivan chuckled, "I didn't see that. So talk to me, Mark. Tell me about the concert you went to after you got back from Tel Aviv."

So I started talking about the Moody Blues show my family and I went to last August. It was hot as hell that day. I'd give anything to go back—to stop whatever break happened between me and Zippy from happening. I told Sivan all about the show—the lights, the effects, the crowd. I went song by song, describing it in every detail. Sivan just kept listening. I didn't know if she was really interested, or if she just wanted to keep me talking.

Sivan stuck with me till the other M-Gangers returned. I was actually sad to hear the coms crackle and Amir announce that he and Sheri were both here to take over Het duties together. He also told Sivan that the chaperones had said I could get dinner once this patrol round was over.

That at least put a bit of a smile on my face. I picked up speed and rounded the corner. There was the same chain-link fence I'd passed a dozen times tonight. The same bunch of sad runaway kids were there huddled around a barrel with a fire built in it. I scanned all of their faces. Nope, no sign of-

Thud!!! Out of nowhere, this giant arm jerked me completely off the ground and slammed me into the wall. I tried to do a standard Krav pluck, but it did no good. I recognized my assailant's voice before I could even focus my eyes on him.

"Cohen??? Mark Cohen??? What in heaven's name are you doing out here???"

It was Mr. Jacobs. DAMN!!! He'd said something

about going "soul-winning" in some poorer areas of town this week. Why did it have to be THIS neighborhood??? I tried to struggle against him, but he started dragging me, "Come on. I'm taking you home to your parents. Have you got any idea what happens in areas like this??? And why are you dressed like-"

I wrestled one arm free and hit the coms, shouting "Amelek, Amelek." I couldn't let Jacobs blow everything. In a split second, I made a choice. I launched into him. I boxed his ears, which made him completely let go of me. Then I transitioned my hands into an eye-gouge, holding him in place for a couple of groin kicks before he could throw me off. I recovered and punched the side of his throat. He stumbled for a second, then tackled me football style, ramming me right back into the wall behind us.

I slammed my forearm into his nose. Blood splattered everywhere.

At that point, I could see Amir and Sheri running towards us from one side. Sivan was coming in from the other side. Sheri had a stun gun, and was already firing it as she ran. It made a horrible crackling noise. But to me, it was somehow comforting to know that in about 3 seconds, Jacobs wasn't going to be resisting any more.

I threw a stomp-kick right into his chest, launching him back a few feet. "Get him!!! Get him!!!" I shouted. But Sheri charged in on me instead.

I remember her making a stabbing motion right at me.

I started to try and say, "No, it's me. There's the target right there." But every muscle in my body exploded in pain. The burning, screaming, tightness and agony shot through every bit of me. I couldn't control a muscle. I couldn't scream. I just had to hope she'd recognize me and stop.

. . . okay, Sheri stop now . . . It's me, Cohen . . . please stop . . . it hurts . . . Sheri?

I got confused. Where was I? Why wouldn't the pain

stop?

What was . . .

Sunday, February 3, 1991, 1:15 a.m.

I woke up shaking. I was crumpled up next to the heater in the safe-house. And I was all alone. I tried to get up, but my arms wouldn't move right. They felt numb like they'd both gone to sleep on me, but they also hurt and when I tried to move them, it hurt worse. I managed to get myself up to mostly a sitting position.

Where was everybody? How did I get here? For a few minutes, I couldn't even remember what happened. Then it started coming back to me: the mission, Mr. Jacobs, Sheri hitting me with a stun-gun . . . but that shouldn't have done this to me. What happened??

The door burst open and Sheri came stomping through, "Get off my back Katzav!!!"

Sivan followed, "Not until you at least explain yourself. What the hell was that out there?!?!?"

"Teaching Cohen a lesson!!!"

"What the hell, Sheri?!?!?! You do NOT hurt teammates like that, especially in the field."

"Yeah, says the girl who ordered Dagan to knock Cohen's head sideways in Tel Aviv."

Sivan's face darkened, "That was wrong of me, and you know it. I regretted it immediately and I've regretted it ever since. Are you so stupid that you have to adopt all of my regrets for your own?"

For a moment, Sheri looked like she was going to hit Sivan. But that would have been the biggest mistake of her life—and possibly the last. And Sheri knew it too. She just whispered back, "I don't have any regrets."

"Dammit Sheri," Sivan grabbed the stun-gun out of Sheri's hand, "This is a WEAPON!!! It's not a toy for you to go around zapping the boys with. You might have seriously hurt Cohen"

"I hope I did."

Sivan was taken aback, "What the hell, Sheri??? What did he ever do to you?"

"Cohen knows what he did. And I'm going to make him pay for it. That thing I did out there was just the beginning."

Sivan's voice lowered to a whisper, "You hurt him again, and I'll do the same to you."

Sheri's voice came to the same whisper, "Then you'll deal with Dagan because she's with me."

Sivan stood there, stunned. Sheri stormed out of the room. What the hell had I ever done to Sheri??? I thought we were friends.

"Don't try to move too quickly, Mark." Sivan came over and put her arm around me. "Sheri hit you with a stun gun. And she kept it on you for a good 90 seconds before anyone realized what she was doing." She looked absolutely disgusted, "And nobody made her stop until I shoved her off of you."

"S- s- so- wh- wh- why am I st- st- still shiv- v-vering???"

She put her finger on my lips to tell me to hush. "Remember our training. A two-second stun-gun blast will incapacitate you. After four seconds, you're disoriented and helpless. You don't know where you are or even who you are. After about ten seconds . . . Mark, she hit you for 90 seconds nonstop. You're going to be a bit shaky for a while."

"Wh- wh- why d- d- di- did sh-"

"I don't know. She thinks you've done something. I don't know what. Now stop trying to talk until you get all your movement back."

Sivan sat there with me and held me for a good half hour while the NSA guys were notified about Jacobs. They took him out the back door in a secret convoy while the chaperones tried to round up the kids. We were all going to head back to M-Gang headquarters, where we were going to figure out what to do with Jacobs.

Finally, I tried to stand up. But my ankles felt wobbly. So did my knees. I had these horrible chills and my first attempt to stand up resulted in Sivan catching me and slowly guiding me back to the floor.

The chaperones walked in and looked unapprovingly at Sivan.

Brice walked over and tried to shoe Sivan off, but she just glared back at him like she was about to kill. Brice tried to motivate me, "Come on Cohen. Get up and shake it off, son." He helped me to my feet, with considerable assistance from Sivan. Both Brice and Cheryl seemed really irritated with me for not being able to move my legs.

The worry on Sivan's face watching me take my first few steps did not give me much confidence, "I'll be right here, Mark."

But Brice was getting impatient, "Enough coddling. Walk it off, Cohen. We haven't got all night." As soon as I could take five steps without stumbling, he was ready to usher us all out into the night.

CHAPTER TWELVE – ALONE AGAIN

We left as a huge group. The NSA guys took Mr. Jacobs out the back door to their secret van, and sped off. That left 10 of us walking out the front door like a tourist group . . . in the middle of downtown Dallas in the middle of the night. We all ran across the street together. My half-running half-hobbling attempts to keep up had Sivan worried. I honestly didn't know how I was going to make it five miles back to the Jewish Community Center. I was already freezing again by the time we got across the street. Zippy and Rachael flagged down some taxis.

Thank God!!! I didn't think I could stand more than a few minutes in this weather. Three taxis pulled over to our little convoy. Two of them were big van-like taxis. The other was a little car.

Rachael, Amir, Danny and Sheri got in the car. Zippy, Aaron, and the adult chaperones got into one of the vans. The other van, sensing that he wasn't going to be making any money off this crowd, zoomed off.

Sivan and I walked over to the van, and saw that there was only one seat. I told Sivan to take it, and ran over to the car. But the car was packed. They couldn't take another passenger.

So I ran back to the van and said "we'll need to squeeze two into this middle seat." But the driver, a guy in his 20s with a thick mideastern Indian accent, shook his finger at me shouting "Nooo, only one more."

Sivan looked at me and said "take it Cohen. You've been freezing out here all night."

I shook my head, "I can't let you stay here by yourself."

Zippy popped her head out, "would ONE of you please get in here so we can go?!?!?"

Sivan insisted, but I couldn't leave a girl alone in the middle of downtown Dallas by herself at midnight--not even one as deadly as Sivan.

"Fine," Zippy snorted "we'll meet you back at M-Gang." She slammed the door shut and motioned for the driver to head on.

Sivan and I stood there dumbfounded. Our "team" was leaving us behind on the side of the street. They drove off in well-heated cars leaving the two of us shivering in the cold.

What!!! The!!! Hell!!! As the cars drove off, I felt a burning feeling in my tummy and a tightness in my throat. Did that really just happen? Did they really just go off and leave us? For a brief moment, a terrible sadness felt like it was going to crush me. This was my gang. These were my closest friends. And they were leaving me behind.

"You're an idiot, Cohen!" This had been Sivan's signature phrase last summer. She'd said it at least once a day. "If I didn't feel so damned sorry for you after this evening's activities, I'd smack the crap out of you right now."

She walked out to the middle of the street, watching the taxis turn a corner several blocks away. She snorted, then turned around and marched right up to me, literally right in my face. "You think you're being honorable, or a gentleman or whatever by sticking by me??? You're not escorting me. You're not going to protect me from anything . . . you're giving me someone I need to protect besides myself!!!"

Sivan was getting really worked up at this point. She grabbed me by the arm and we started walking. "And you're not taking basic damned care of yourself!! You've been out in the freezing cold all night. You've been in a physical confrontation. You took 90-seconds worth of a stun-gun blast. You're dehydrated. And you haven't eaten anything in 15 hours."

By now, she was outright shouting. "You still shivering from the stun-gun. You should be seeing a medic or going to the hospital. And now you're going to walk 5 miles in the freezing cold. Idiot!!!" She stopped dead in her tracks and spun around to face me again. "Tsipporah taught you to stand up for yourself. So why can't you stand up to Tsipporah? You just let her walk all over you."

She turned around and kept going, dragging me by the arm. "Idiot!!!"

That's when we heard him, "Excuse me . . . you there." We both turned around to face him: Andy Moore, Benson's Dallas-area grab-guy. "I'm lost. Are you two kids from around here?"

Yeah, I'm sure he was. I was supposed to fight this guy off? My muscles still didn't right work from the stun-gun blast. And this guy was going to go through his entire kidnap script with us.

Sivan sighed, "I haven't got time for the song and dance." She had her gun out, cocked, and pointed at his face before I could even blink. He just stood there.

After a few seconds, he tried to smooth his way out of this, "Listen, kids. I'm just a guy who's lost and-"

"And you were going to kidnap some more kids for Stanley Benson. Hi. I'm Sivan Katzav. I'm one of the decoy kids the Federal Government hired to catch you. Unfortunately, my cover is now blown and the capture team is sleeping on the job, so I'm going to take you in myself. Move and I start shooting. When my clip is empty, I reload and keep shooting. I stop shooting you when I run out of bullets, and I've got about five clips on me right now. Do you understand?"

He just stared at her dumbfounded.

"And in case you don't believe this gun is real," BANG!!! She shot the ground right by his feet, then aimed the gun right back at his mid-section. "Any questions?"

He shook his head no. I think he was still so shocked at this turn of events that he wouldn't have known how to respond anyway.

"Good. Now, on your knees."

He dropped to his knees.

"Mark, cuff him. Mr. Moore, if you so much as twitch, you know what I will do." She had slowly stepped towards him so that she was just out of his reach, but could not possibly miss if she fired.

I walked over and cuffed him. Sivan ordered him to lay down face first on the ground. Then she walked over, slung the backpack off her shoulder and pulled out a syringe. "This is called Ketamine, Mr. Moore. It's going to make you sleepy." She injected it into his arm. "I suggest you don't fight it."

Fortunately, we hadn't made it far in our little walk before he found us—the downtown safe house was still just around the corner. So we dragged him back, dead asleep, and chained his cuffed hands to the table, just in case he woke back up some time this year.

Then we headed back out into the night. Sivan hadn't spoken since injecting Moore with the Ketamine. About two blocks later, Sivan saw a taxi-van and ran to flag it down. I ran after her, but my legs were just so tight and weak. I could barely move. Every joint ached.

Finally!!!! We got into the van. Sivan gave the driver directions to the Jewish Community Center, then crawled over to the back seat with me.

After pausing for what felt like an eternity, she finally spoke "I couldn't leave you there alone. We never leave a teammate behind. It's wrong. And . . . I already did this to you once. You remember?"

I shook my head no. "You've always stuck-"

"In Tel Aviv. When everything went wrong. We fled to the rendezvous point, but left you and Tsipporah alone to face that crowd."

Oh, that's what she meant.

"I felt sick for hours. We sent a team back in to extract the two of you, but they couldn't find you. Then it seemed like forever. We waited and waited, but nobody could find you. Tsipporah finally called from that cafe at Dizengoff, but before we could get to you, a team of Black Card soldiers stopped us and said that a terrorist team had hit that cafe."

I never really thought about what that evening had been like for the other M-Gangers. It must have kinda sucked for them--waiting and not knowing. But I never really thought about it.

"Hang on a minute," she leaned over the seat, "Mr. Driver, could you take us to the pancake house on Lemon."

I felt kinda embarrassed, but I had to state the obvious, "Sivan, I don't have any money."

She looked at me like I was speaking a foreign language, then pulled a HUGE roll of $20s out of her backpack. "My imeh always makes sure I'm never stranded."

We went into the pancake house, and Sivan offered the driver $100 to just sit out in the parking lot and wait for us. We went in and took our time. She ordered me a HUGE dinner, which I really appreciated since I hadn't eaten since yesterday at noon. Over the next hour, we talked about EVERYTHING: concerts we'd been to, TV shows we liked, bands . . . everything except M-Gang and missions. It was great.

But when we got back into the taxi, Sivan reverted back to a more unfortunate subject.

"I still can't believe you killed Hasan."

I really wish people would stop bringing that up. "Yeah well, he had the drop on Zippy. He was gonna shoot-"

"This I know already. She's told me many times." Sivan smiled. "I don't understand why she's being so . . . pissy . . . is this the word?"

"Yeah, it's close enough."

"Pissy with you. I don't understand this. She loves you. She spent a long time outright obsessing over you. Then you saves her life and she just turned hard towards you." She sat back. "She even left you behind tonight . . . twice." Sivan sighed. "I don't want to have her in the room when I . . . interview your teacher."

"Interview Mr. Jacobs? Why?"

She smirked, "He's going to be our new chaperone. He doesn't know it yet. Nobody knows it yet. But he's about to replace Brice and Cheryl."

Sivan's eyes turned dark just as we pulled into the JCC parking lot, "I've had it with those damned tourists. Did you see them just driving off without us?"

I nodded.

A slight grin pierced her face, "They're finished. When we get inside, I will show those two worthless windbags where the fish pisses from."

Uh oh. I'd heard her use that term before. Someone was about to bleed.

CHAPTER THIRTEEN – WHERE THE FISH PISSES FROM

I'd seen Zippy beat someone up before. But she didn't hold a candle to Sivan. Zippy brutally overwhelmed people with a barrage of devastating strikes . . . usually to the privates. But Sivan seemed to be all over her victim in a blur of murderous moves, like a spider repeatedly stinging and wrapping up its prey in a cocoon all at once.

It happened so fast I barely caught it all.

Brice stood up when he saw us walk through the door. He walked over to Sivan, while saying something about "what took you so long?" He extended his arm like he was going to wrap Sivan up in a hug.

She grabbed his wrist and pulled him, while bursting towards him. Her arms shot out like scissors: one hand slapping him HARD in the groin, the other hand simultaneously shooting into his throat. His whole body jolted like it had been short-circuited: should he double over from being struck in the groin, or fly backwards from being struck in the throat? Both her hands immediately became claws. The hand that had slapped his groin immediately grabbed his privates and yanked them forwards with horrifying speed. Sivan's other hand was on his throat, with her fingers digging into his windpipe, shoving him backwards.

She somehow maintained both of these grips while throwing him to the ground. Then she seemed to fall on top of him. Her knee falling right into his face . . . with all her body weight.

Splat!!! Blood went everywhere. His whole body lurched into the fetal position.

Before anyone could react, Sivan was across the room: one hand crushing Cheryl's throat in a terrifying vice-grip, the other one across her face with Sivan's fingers digging deep into her eye sockets.

Zippy and Rachael sprinted towards Sivan, but they were too late. Sivan tossed Cheryl across the room by her throat. Cheryl landed right next to Brice, who was rolling around on the floor, moaning in horrible agony.

Sivan spun around, facing Zippy and Rachael. They both stopped dead in their tracks. Sivan had not even broken a sweat. "I dislocated Brice's balls, and probably blinded Cheryl for life." She drew the gun from behind her hip and cocked it. "Does anyone have a problem with that?"

They both stood there, stunned. Nobody had ever seen Sivan lose it before. She could be the most sullen person on earth. Yeah. She could be a monster in sparring. Yeah. But she'd never really hurt anyone before today.

Zippy smiled and put her hands up as if asking Sivan to calm down, "It's okay Katzav. I never liked either of them very much anyway."

After a few tense seconds, she seemed to calm down a bit. Zippy and Rachael both backed away, and returned to the other M-Gangers in the lounge. Nobody had spoken a word.

Sivan went over to the phone and picked it up, tapping

the numbers with her gun, "Sanders, this is Katzav. One of Benson's minions is unconscious and handcuffed to a table in our downtown safe room . . . no, in the DOWNTOWN safe room, not at M-Gang headquarters . . . WHY? Glad you asked. Our TEAM couldn't capture him because the TEAM, including those two idiots you hired, abandoned me and Mark downtown. The minion tried to kidnap us both once we were alone and uncovered. We neutralized him and left him there because we couldn't effectively capture him with only two people."

She looked at the other M-Gangers like she was ready to kill them. Zippy looked like she had just been punched in the stomach. Sivan continued, "I just fired your actors. You should probably send an ambulance for them. And you should hurry before I decide to upgrade their ride from ambulance to hearse. We don't tolerate BETRAYAL at M-Gang!!!" She slammed the phone down and glared at Zippy for a brief eternity.

"You still think you can lead this group?" Sivan asked.

"You still think Cohen should be part of it?" Zippy responded.

I felt like someone had stabbed me in the heart. Zippy really wanted me out of M-Gang, and Sivan was the one keeping me in. How the hell did that happen? I felt sick. I wanted to run out the door. I wanted to cry. I wanted to scream.

Sivan turned and walked towards Brice and Cheryl, "Don't mess with me, Dagan. You screwed us tonight. Not just me and Mark. You screwed the entire team." She stopped for a second, "You screwed the MISSION. Whatever problems you have with Cohen are YOUR problems. Sort them out." She leaned over Brice's crumpled body and said something about them being fired, and if she ever saw either of them again they would know such suffering as to make this evening seem like a paper-cut. The NSA guys showed up a few minutes later, and after what seemed like endless talk, they agreed with Sivan. The adults had left two kids on the side of the road. They were lucky it was Sivan and not her mom that had beaten them up. Everyone agreed that it would be best if nobody ever told Sivan's mom about what happened. Both the chaperones ended up in an ambulance tonight.

If Sivan's mom knew about them leaving us on the side of the road . . . better to not think of such horrors. But it made no difference to me. I never saw either of them again.

Around 3 in the morning, after a painfully long closed door meeting with the adults, Sivan emerged with a big smile on her face. "I get to go recruit the Bible teacher. He's going to replace the 'chaperone' tourists."

Zippy looked both shocked and disgusted, "So now instead of two little idiots, we have one big one?"

Sivan chuckled, "Well . . . this one is going to get a PROPER introduction. There'll be no question as to who is in charge of who."

"And how can you be sure?"

Sivan smirked, "I'm going to make him bleed. I'm going to shove a gun in his mouth and beat him till he pisses himself. The adults think we should make him 'go missing' for a few days, then turn up having been 'mugged' and not remembering much about it. So if you'll all excuse me, I have some hitting to do."

She went to the girl's bathroom and changed into some official looking clothes. When she returned, she looked like an adult agent. She even had on her official NSA badge. "Time for some fun." She said, heading down the hallway.

Once Sivan had closed the door, Zippy came over to me and said, "Looks like you can still manage to find a girl to save you . . . pathetic."

I wasn't going to let this get to me, "Well, at least I never left anyone behind."

Zippy didn't seem fazed by my comment either, "I've

never left behind anyone who was worth sticking by." She looked directly at my face, "Why don't you leave M-Gang before you get someone I care about killed?" She walked away before I could say anything back. A few minutes later I heard Mr. Jacobs begging for his life at the top of his lungs through the door. That put a smile on my face.

I really hated that guy.

CHAPTER FOURTEEN – THEY'VE FOUND US

Tuesday, February 5, 1991, 5:00 p.m.

Asma forced the door open, dropping her grocery bag and spilling her newly-purchased produce all across the floor. "Damn," she muttered. Why the hell did she and Yusef still live in this hell-hole of a condo? The damned lock never worked right. It was a fight getting it to close. It was a fight getting it to open. She had complained to the management group, but never got anywhere.

"Eliana" she shouted, "can you come help mommy?"

She kicked a few of the fallen apples into the foyer and slammed the door behind her. Her new black boots made such a loud clicking noise every time she stepped on the hard wood floor.

"Eliana, mommy's home!!" Maybe the kid was in the bathroom. But the condo felt unnaturally empty. Even the process of dropping the half empty grocery bags on the counter seemed to create a canyon's worth of echoes through the place.

"Eliana, get down here please!!" She was growing impatient. She threw off her jacket, swiped the TV remote, and turned it on with one graceful move. "Should have been a ballerina," she thought to herself as she danced over to pick up the fallen produce. She was right. Her

figure was perfect for the ballet. And she was only 32, so maybe there was still time to . . . nah, she was too successful to switch careers now.

The television was blaring something about a private school teacher going missing. Asma usually let herself get lost in the day's stories while putting up her groceries. But today was different. She felt uneasy about something. Something just wasn't right. She looked over at the television. They were showing a photograph of the missing teacher. Asma felt a sudden sadness. The man looked like Arnold Schwarzenegger. If a man who's that built is missing, someone probably shot him. Maybe a street gang. Who knows? In a week or two, there would probably be a story about his body being found in some rural dump. That's how these stories always ended. At least the news was showing something other than Israelis practicing for chemical attacks.

That was all the news had shown for the past week. Ever since the Kuwait invasion last summer, the news had been obsessed with war in the middle-east. They were calling it "Desert Shield." What a joke . . . "shield!!" Asma had seen her fill of middle-eastern war. She'd seen enough for two lifetimes. The only people hiding behind a "shield" are the ones who caused the misery to begin with. Damned Iraqis. She wondered how many of her people would suffer for the actions of this madman. After all, the Arabs with no nation of their own always suffered whenever a rogue Arab did something like this.

And these days, the news was showing nothing but Israelis worrying about their precious safety. Asma was absolutely sick of it. Those . . people . . would gladly murder her, her husband, and little Eliana--despite the fact that the child was only six years old.

A sudden horror came over her. Where the hell is Eliana?

Asma didn't even shout. The condo was simply too silent. She bolted up the stairs in a mix of fear and rage - the thunderous sound of her boots hitting each stair ringing through the condo like angry war drums. Where was she? What if she never made it home? We knew six was too young for little Ellie to join the latch-key kid generation!!!!! What if someone got to her??? What if she was . . .

Asma's horror exploded when she got to the top stair. Eliana was nowhere to be found. There was no sign that she had even been home.

Asma couldn't breathe. She could barely mutter out desperate prayers in Arabic while running downstairs to the phone. Someone had Eliana. Someone had her baby!!!!!

She dialed Yusef as fast as she could and waited . . . ring . . . pick up the phone . . . ring . . . pick up, dammit . . . ring . . . oh god, what if something happened to him too? His work was top secret. If anyone had learned what he was doing, he would be a target. Savak, Mossad, MI6 . . . all those names that frightened her . . . all those boogiemen . . . and now one of them had her little Eliana.

. . . ring . . . "hello."

"YUSEF it's me!!! Eliana's-"

"We know, Mrs. Hadawi. Please calm down."

That wasn't Yusef's voice. It took her a full ten seconds of confusion to put together her next few words.

"Who . . . who is this?"

"This is Special Agent Jeremy Sanders, U.S. National Security Agency. Agents are on their way to your house as we speak. We will get your daughter back, Mrs. Hadawi. Please don't panic. We're already working on it."

She couldn't speak. She only knew that she dropped the phone because it bounced off her boot and went spinning on the floor.

The National Security Agency? What the hell was happening? Just ten minutes ago, her biggest worry was getting dinner finished before Yusef got home, and maybe catching the Arsenio Hall Show before bed. Now, one of those scary names was coming to visit her. The National Security Agency. Worse yet, she would need their help.

Her legs went out from under her.

THUD. She didn't even feel the pain as her body hit the floor. She let out the horrific howl of a mother who's just lost her baby. Her screams would have had the neighbors dialing 911, if any had been home to hear.

She looked helplessly at the television, getting one last look at the missing Arnold lookalike. The sadness she had for him and his family was gone. It was her family now. It was her little Eliana. It was her baby. A final sickening thought went through her head before she completely fainted . . . they've found us.

CHAPTER FIFTEEN – SCORCHED EARTH

Thursday, February 7, 1991, 7:15 p.m.

The eight of us sat in the M-Gang conference room. We'd been called in for an emergency meeting. Normally, we'd do a little training on a Thursday, then take the rest of the night to do whatever we wanted. Although lately, we weren't hanging out much. We'd just disperse after training.

But every one of us got a call today saying that we'd have an emergency group meeting tonight around seven. So here we were.

Sanders came bursting through the door, "Our mission just went critical. We need your team to prepare for a violent extraction." He always sounded so technical when discussing such things.

Zippy spoke up first, "What's changed? We caught Moore, didn't we?" She had a lot of nerve saying "we." Sivan and I caught Moore. Zippy sat on her backside.

Sanders sighed, "Moore doesn't know anything. We

now believe that the anonymous tip we received was from someone in Benson's organization. It was Benson's way of firing Moore." He paused for a second, "I still haven't received clearance to share this with you kids, but its mission critical. You all understand?"

We all nodded.

He continued, "Stanley Benson isn't just into human trafficking. He's also working closely with terrorist groups in the West Bank, Jordan, Lebanon, and Syria. He doesn't just funnel money, he helps them with . . . how should I say this . . . ransom missions."

We all just stared at him. Zippy said "Don't spare our feelings Sanders. Get to it."

"Well . . . there have been a few incidents over the past decade where Hamas and Hizbollah teams have attempted to kidnap and ransom family members of certain individuals in the U.S. to make them do things."

Sivan cut him off, "We know this already."

"Yes, well. Benson's group just kidnapped a six year old child. We've known for some time that Benson's group intended to kidnap this child. We tried to shadow the family without letting them know they were in danger."

Sivan snorted, "Yeah, you're good at not giving any warning, aren't you?"

Sanders seemed annoyed, "Look, we're not Mossad. We work differently. Our methods may be different but they usually work. Benson just managed to get past us. Alright? Now we're relying on you kids to get the little girl back. You think you can manage that? Her father works for a government contractor. They're designing a new system to protect nations like . . oh . . ISRAEL from rocket attacks. Now, if we operated like Mossad, our next move would be to kill the father before he could be made to hand over any information. We're not Mossad. We want you kids to go in, rescue the little girl, and if possible, take a few prisoners so we can get information from them."

Zippy sighed, "Give us the file on the family."

Sanders handed Zippy a file, "The little girl's name is Eliana Hadawi. Her father works for Ray-tech industries. He's a design-"

SLAM!!! Zippy threw the file on the floor. The papers scattered everywhere.

"Is there a problem, Ms. Dagan?"

"Get someone else to do it."

"Excuse me?"

"Get someone else to do it. Our team won't be getting involved. We can help you find and kill Benson, but we're not going to rescue the kid."

Sanders's jaw was on the ground. Mine was too. I don't think any of us could believe what we were hearing. Sanders was certainly shocked. "Dagan, we could do that ourselves. We need M-Gang because our analysts say you're the best chance we have of getting the kid back alive."

"Then the kid dies." Zippy sounded so cold that it scared me.

Sivan stepped in front of Sanders, "Look . . . mister, give me a minute . . . give us a minute to discuss this. Okay?"

Sanders hesitated, but he left the room. Sivan immediately spun around, "What the hell, Dagan?!?!?"

"Hadawi!!!! Hadawi!!! They want us to rescue to someone named Hadawi!!! They want us to put our lives to danger for someone named Hadawi. I may be many stupid things, Katzav. But I have my limits, and I'LL BE DAMNED if I'm going to put my life in danger for a damned Palestinian!!!"

"Zippy, she's an innocent child."

"She is Palestinian child!!!"

"Zippy, for the thousandth time the Palestinians aren't the bad guys, the Hamas and Hizbollah among them are."

"Spare to me the sentimental nonsense, Sivan. You weren't there when 'innocent' Palestinian children were throwing rocks at me and Mark."

"Zippy, you can't let last year make you a monster! You have to protect the innocent. That's why my aba-"

Zippy interrupted, "Your aba was Mossad, just like mine!!! And they did no to forget that they were IDF before that, and-"

"Tsippi, my aba helped found the COGAT initiative. You know this. His unit commander gave humanitarian aid to non-combatant Palestinians, and he nearly persuaded the IDF to use his unit as a blueprint for all IDF units. You know this!!! My aba devoted years to protecting the innocent among them from the killers among them." Sivan was shouting now.

"And where did this get him??? They murder him just the same!!! You should remember. You watched it happen!!!"

We all gasped. I didn't know this about Sivan. From the looks on everyone else's faces, none of the other M-Gangers did either. Sivan looked back at Zippy like she wanted to hit her. Zippy had just betrayed a deep trust, and Sivan's face said it. Zippy's did too. She stepped backwards a bit, like she knew she'd just gone too far and done something she could never take back.

For an instant, Sivan flinched like she was going to lash out at Zippy. But instead she just whispered, "They never made him a monster. And they will never make me a monster. I will not shame his memory like that. What are you going to do? Can you still tell the innocent from the killers, or do you just call them all 'Palestinian' and let God sort them out? Are you this protector of life you keep claiming to be, or are you the angel of death—the monster that you've been afraid of becoming? You know the killers are after this family. We have a chance to get the real bad guys and save a small child. What are you going to do?"

Zippy completely backed down and Sivan invited Sanders back into the room.

"I'm glad to see you've had a change of heart, Dagan. You are free to plan the mission however you desire, and you can train however you'd like, but I want to be kept in the loop."

Zippy nodded, "Understood."

"Now, you'll have your adult chaperone for the entire period. I spoke to Mr. Jacobs earlier today. He was actually quite cooperative. He seemed to be worried that we'd send the 'devil child' in to get him."

We all looked over at Sivan, who innocently shrugged, saying "What?"

Sanders continued, "If Benson didn't know that we were after him, he knows now. So we really need to hurry. What's the soonest you guys can prep a mission."

Sivan responded, "We need three weeks to prep an extraction, if we're going to do it right—depending on how good your intelligence work is. If we have to do the ground work, add another week. I know it's not as quick as you'd like. But that's what we need, if we're going to do it right. Do you have any leads on Benson?"

"We don't have any direct leads. You have all our intelligence information in the file that Ms. Dagan just scattered all over the floor. But three weeks is out of the question."

Zippy piped up, "Then we train harder for whatever time we have."

Sanders cracked his awkward smile, "Good, then we're on. Dagan, you're still the leader of this bunch. Who do you want for your alpha team?"

Zippy looked at Sivan, "I want Aaron to be my right-hand. We figure out Aleph and Beit designations later. I want Sheri and Danny to be Het and Ayin. Rachael should train with us to substitute for me or Aaron if needs-be. Amir should train to substitute for Sheri or Danny."

The damned Zippy/Aaron clique strikes again.

She continued, "Sivan should check over all our

operational plans. We need a second set of eyes on everything. We need about three weeks to plan a decent operation but, since we don't have that . . ." She paused as though she was getting lost in thought.

Sanders inquired, "What about Cohen."

"Cohen sits this one out. If I have to rescue some kid who's going to grow up to throw rocks at me, at least I'm not going to have any dead weight on my team."

I was stunned. She had some real gumption. Zippy wasn't protecting me anymore. She really wanted me out of M-Gang.

She kept going, "He doesn't even train with us. Training for this needs to be individualized anyway." She looked over at me with an icy gloat as if to say, "I win."

Sanders just nodded, "Got it. Cohen sits out." He sounded almost like a doctor, taking notes during an examination.

I turned and left. The knot in my throat was going to get the best of me. Tears were welling up. If I said one damned word, I was going to cry. I made it out the door just in time for Sivan to catch me yelling "Mark, slow down!!!"

She could tell how upset I was. I couldn't even think up words to say.

"Mark, you've got to stand up to her. You've got to confront her."

"Oh yeah, like that's going to help." Here it came, I was starting to cry.

"Mark, I don't know what her problem is, but I can't fight your fights for you. I'm not her. I'm not a 'bodyguard' type." She was getting worked up. "Look, I want to confront her about how she's treating you, but it's not my place. It's yours. I will back you up. But I won't do it unless you first stand up for yourself. You have to stand up to her."

"I don't want to fight her!!! I just want her to be the

way she was!!!"

"What EITHER of us wants is IRRELEVANT!!! This is what we're stuck with!!!"

Sivan had never shouted at me before. It took her a second to calm back down. "I will not fight for someone who does not fight for himself. Stand up to her."

With that, she turned around and went back into the JCC. I eventually followed, going into the lobby to call my mom. This was really going to test my ability to keep my mouth shut. I told my mom I wasn't feeling well, which wasn't too far from the truth. I could never tell her that I was having trouble with anyone at M-Gang.

A few months ago, one of my classmates at Collins prank-called our house one Saturday afternoon. My dad sat me down and demanded to know "Is it happening again???" My parents were convinced that I brought all the terrible things that happened last spring on myself. If I started having problems with people at Collins or at M-Gang, it would just confirm what my parents already suspected: the problem was 100% me!!!

Still, when your best friend turns on you, it's a little hard to keep quiet when your mom asks "what's wrong?" Fortunately, a bunch of Mossad agents taught me the skills necessary to insist that "Nothing is wrong. I just don't feel well. I think I'm coming down with something." More importantly, they taught me to make it believable.

CHAPTER SIXTEEN – A SILVER LINING

Thursday, February 14, 1991, 4:15 p.m.

I was sitting in the student lounge at Collins, staring out the window. I didn't want to speak to anyone. A week of no M-Gang . . . with the way Zippy had been treating me lately, you'd think this would improve things. But it only felt worse.

Partly because it was just now beginning to hit me. I spent much of the last week in bed. Last Friday morning, I woke up with a sore throat, fever, and a horrible cough. All that time out in the cold finally got to me. I caught the full-blown flu. Today was my first day back at school, and I still felt pretty sick.

It delayed my having to explain to my parents why I was spending so much time at home and away from M-Gang, but it just made it harder for me today. Today was the first day I'd gone to school in months without knowing there was Krav training or some other M-Gang activity at the end of the tunnel. Today, there was nothing. It hurt. That "nothing" felt like I was starving, and there was no food to be had.

The fact that I still felt a little less than half alive made it easier for me to avoid talking to any of my classmates. How could I tell them that I'd been a real-live James Bond, and now I was being shut-out . . . that I was just a kid again—at least for three weeks. It scared me, but I was also deeply afraid that this isolation would not end on the fourth week. Zippy seemed ready to shut me out of her life forever.

It was a dreary grey afternoon—raining constantly, but not really storming. The weather reflected my feelings perfectly. My week with the flu had given me a chance to catch up watching Dark Shadows. It was a remake of an old TV series about vampires. It came on every Saturday night, so I've had my VCR set to tape it for a month now. I just never got a chance to watch any of it until I got sick.

Before meeting Zippy and joining M-Gang, being home from school for a week and watching TV nonstop would have been my idea of heaven. Now, it just made me itchy. I wanted to be working out. I wanted to be getting my training going.

I kept watching the parking lot's entrance as though I expected my mother to turn in any minute now. But I really knew better. It was only 4pm. She never got here to pick me up before 4:30.

As I watched, a "bullet" van turned into the parking lot. I recognized it immediately. It swung around to the front of the building. I got up and walked out the door into the rain. The van's door opened. Sivan jumped out and ran over to me, carrying her traditional black backpack.

"Hi Mark."

"Sivan, what are you doing here? Shouldn't you be working with-"

"Miss Impossible???" she asked, looking over her shoulder at the van. "I can only stay for a minute. I have to get back to that nightmare."

"Is it really that bad?"

She nodded, "Without you to beat-up on, Tsipporah has been lashing out at everyone. She's even turned on Aaron. He told Rachael he plans to quit once this mission is over."

Wow. That might make my life a bit better. Sivan must have seen the smile creeping onto my face. "He's a good guy, Mark. In fact, Tsipporah has been pretty horrible to him since you've been gone. Everything she did to you she's been doing to him. But it's not just her. There's something wrong with everyone in in the group. I don't know what's turning us all against each other, but I don't like it."

I shrugged, "me neither."

"I was supposed to call you this weekend and give you an assignment directly from my mom. She wants you to start meeting with Mr. Jacobs during lunch-time. Your cover story is that your grades have slipped, and he's tutoring you one-on-one."

"In BIBLE class???"

Now it was her turn to shrug, "These are religious people. He could be saving your soul. Your real job is to brief him on M-Gang, Mossad . . . generally letting him know what he's gotten himself into. Tell him about the missions you went on in Israel. Explain the current mission to him."

"But isn't he supposed to be getting his orders directly from Sanders."

She smiled, "Tell him this comes directly from me. He's more afraid of me than he is of Sanders," she started to laugh, "but if he wets himself at the mention of my name, you're on your own." We both laughed.

She reached out and caressed my face, "It's been too long since anyone has really seen you smile or laugh." She took my hand and led me back into the building. "I've got something for you."

She dug down into her bag, "Here it is. Tsipporah said you hate Valentine's Day." Ouch, the wretched name alone made me cringe—the dreaded V word. "She said last year a bunch of kids sent extremely cruel notes to you and hurt you." She looked up, "And the events of the last few weeks probably didn't make this one very happy for you either. But I thought maybe I could make it just a little better."

She handed me a small package. I recognized it immediately and gasped. "Sivan, how'd you know???"

"Tsipporah was talking about getting you this for Hanukah before she turned all mean. I wanted you to have it." She hugged me tightly. "Happy Valentine's Day, Mark."

"Happy Valentine's Day, Sivan." I started to tear-up again, "Thank you."

She ran back over to her mom's van and hopped in. She rolled down the window and stuck her head out for a second, "My mom and I are coming over to your house tomorrow night. She has something she'd like to discuss with your parents. And I have some stuff I'd like to talk to you about." With that, she rolled the window back up and they drove off.

I took the package and slipped it into my jacket pocket before anyone could see it and confiscate it as "devil worshipping" material. Sivan had given me a cassette of Boston's "Third Stage" album. It was the best Valentine ever.

Part Three – Never More to Go Astray

CHAPTER SEVENTEEN – A MIDNIGHT SUMMIT

Saturday, February 16, 1991

"No Sivan!!! Run!!! Ruuuuuuuu-BANG!!!"

She woke up in a cold sweat, panting. A half-second later, she was out of the bed, gun in hand. In a single flash, she cocked it and aimed it directly at her bedroom door. She was in a pinpoint perfect shooting stance. She backed up to the wall in a diagonal direction. Her tactical movements would have made a SWAT team jealous. Her eyes scanned the room. There was no danger.

The fear slowly bled out of her. She clicked the safety back onto the gun. Then went through the slow process of removing the magazine, popping the bullet out of the firing chamber, loading it back into the magazine, and reloading her weapon.

She felt absolutely stupid. She could have killed someone. It had been two years since she'd had the nightmare. Why was tonight different? Why was it back? Why was she so jumpy? Hell, if her imeh or her brother had been in the doorway, she might have killed them—over a damned bad dream. Over a ghost in her head.

Something was going terribly wrong. Her friends weren't exactly at each other's throats, but they were coming close. Some unspoken tension seemed to be ripping her safe little circle of people apart. Her brother had tried to hit her. Her best friend, the girl with the messed up hair, had gone from obsessing about "the boy on the playground" to hating him. One of her other friends had attacked "the boy" with a stun gun.

She got up and went downstairs to the kitchen. Her brother was already there. He had a small bowl of hummus and a stack of crackers in front of him. But it didn't look like he'd eaten anything—he just stared at the food.

"Can't sleep sis?"

"Yeah. I had the nightmare again." No need to say anymore. There was only one nightmare deserving to be called "THE nightmare." Sivan had relived the moment of her father's death again.

Amir had been spared the horrific image by a combination of sheer terror and the invisible electric wire running down the insides of his legs that evening. He'd run with everything he had. He had even peed his pants, he was running so hard. But he had heard the bang. "Yeah. You'd think seeing a shrink might fix some of our mental . . . issues."

She sighed, "Yeah. I'm starting to think he's caused more harm than he's solved." She opened the fridge and pulled out a leftover olive tapenade from last night's sandwiches.

"Well, if you want to make an omelet, you've got to break a few eggs."

"But Amir, we're not breaking eggs. We're breaking each other. I can't put my finger on it, but there's something sick going on at M-Gang."

"Yeah. There's something sick alright—your buddy Cohen."

She slammed the refrigerator door! "Not this again, Amir. Don't make me hurt you again." She began the mental process of preparing to hurt him. It made her feel ill—the memory of him trying to punch her, ducking, locking onto him, her knee ramming into his thigh, the cracking sound, the horrified look on his face . . . the second shot . . . the third . . . the sights and sounds of his spirit breaking . . .

"How can you let him treat you like he does?"

"What the hell are you talking about?" She was truly

incredulous. Mark mistreating her? She slid into a chair and snagged on of his crackers.

"I know what he did in Tel Aviv. I know how he used you. I know how he charmed you into making out with him. I know how he just tossed you aside for Dagan. How can you stand to-"

"Amir, where the hell are you getting this crap?"

He looked down, "Don't deny it, sis. I've already been warned that you'd deny it. I've been prepared for this conversation." He looked up at her. "I don't care how much you hurt me. ONE OF US has to watch out for your dignity!!! How can you stand to even look at Cohen after what he did?"

Sivan leaned forward in her chair, crossing her arms against the kitchen table. "Time for you to tell me everything, Amir. Who's been feeding you this nonsense?"

He sat silent.

She breathed a heavy sigh, "I am perfectly capable of MAKING you tell me. Now talk!!! Don't make me twist your balls to get it out of you, because you know I will."

He looked her directly in the eyes. His face had turned red. A single tear streaked down his cheek. But he held back the rage, and started talking . . .

CHAPTER EIGHTEEN – THE INNER SANCTUM

Friday, February 22, 1991, 12:15 p.m.

Mr. Jacobs sat across from me with his mouth open so wide I thought his jaw was going to fall completely off.

". . . then I said 'Akbar this' and I shot him." I hesitated. Why am I sugar-coating this for him? Let's rephrase that, "Actually, I completely emptied the clip into him. I don't remember much after that. A bunch of soldiers arrived and took us away. I started school here about four days later. Are you with me so far?"

He just sat there staring at me. His face was a mix of horror, awe, shock . . . I think he was just completely overwhelmed. Over the past hour, I'd told him about all three of my missions in Israel. But I think it was the shootout at Dizengoff Café that pushed him over the edge.

"Mr. Jacobs, do you have any questions?"

"Um . . . did he die?"

"Hassan? Yeah, I shot him fifteen times, and the IDF guys said every shot was a kill shot. He's very much dead.

But he had killed many people and would have killed many more had I let him live. That's what we do. We kill bad people to keep them from killing innocent people. Are you keeping up?"

"Um . . . yeah, I just- That was the week before school started."

"Yeah. I killed a man, caught a plane, landed, and the very next day I came here to take your 'aptitude' test. Two days later I met you."

"Yeah, but you seemed so . . . normal." He looked dumbfounded.

I sighed, "That's what this is all about. You're off saving the world one day—violently most of the time—and the next day you have to be all 'la-di-da' like you've been sitting at home playing Nintendo games." I kinda understood how much this was bothering him. "It's hard to come down from being the violent monster to being a normal person. It's a lot of work. That time you grabbed me by the lapel during my argument with Frog in study hall . . . I had to really concentrate to keep from doing what my body had been trained to do on autopilot, and puncture your trachea. YOU have to learn that same level of control."

Of course, this was going to be a difficult situation. Yesterday morning, Mr. Jacobs made us all watch a video by some televangelist type named Brother David Dimmet, whom I've decided to forevermore refer to as "David Dimwit." Anyway, Mr. Dimwit has a series of videotapes called "The Ugly Truth about Rock Music," where he talks about demons possessing rock albums, demons possessing people through their headphones, rock musicians being Satan-worshippers, backwards satanic messages in popular music, and a bunch of other stuff that it's hard to repeat with a straight face.

So this morning, Mr. Jacobs decided to allow the class to have a full debate on whether rock music was evil. I took the stand that it wasn't. A bunch of my classmates decided to "fight the good fight" and show me that I was going to burn in hell for listening to Def Leppard.

And here I was a few hours later, telling Mr. Jacobs all about how I "fought the good fight" and killed an international terrorist last summer. Like I said, this was a difficult situation. He'd been fighting a "culture war" against music he didn't like. I'd been fighting a real war against real bad-guys who shoot back.

"So how do you kids train for something like that?"

I explained Krav training to him, and assured him that he'd have a chance to witness some of it himself—even though I couldn't participate at M-Gang for the moment, and had no idea when I'd be allowed back in.

I was going to enjoy these lunchtime discussions. He did ask about the "Upside-Down-Eyelash-Nightmare-Devil-Child." I told him a little bit about her . . . okay, I embellished a little bit. But I left out the part about what she did to the last pair of chaperones. I figured I'd save that story for the next time he tried to tell me that my Boston and Styx albums were going to get me sent to hell.

Like I said, I was really going to enjoy this.

Friday, February 22, 1991, 4:30 p.m.

This afternoon, my heart leapt when I saw that bullet van pull into the Collins parking lot. Last week, Sivan and her mom had come over to my house and discussed her mom's "ideas" with my parents. My dad had done well at his job, so his company was going to send him and my mom to Hawaii for a week-long vacation in March. My parents had arranged for Elise's babysitter to keep us for the week, but Mrs. Katzav had other ideas. She suggested that I could stay at her house with her kids that week.

They were hesitant until she told them that, unlike Elise's babysitter, she wouldn't take any money. That got their attention. They'd still have to pay for Elise, but paying someone to keep one kid was much easier than paying for two.

In return, Mrs. Katzav wanted me to "mentor" and "tutor" Amir with some of his schoolwork. That would have sounded like a joke around this time last year, but with the grades I'd made since joining M-Gang, my parents thought it would be a good way of "giving back." Of course, they had no idea that Amir was a straight-A student. So for the foreseeable future, I was going to be spending my weekends at the Katzav house.

That's where Sivan's ideas came in. She wanted me and Amir to keep up with our Krav training together. She didn't want me getting rusty while Zippy had me shut out. And she didn't think Amir was getting anything out of training now that Zippy was apparently just using their daily training hour to beat the crap out of everyone.

So when that bullet van pulled into the parking lot, this was a moment I'd been waiting more than a week for. I bolted out of the Collins back door and hopped in. We headed over to the Katzav house, which was in one of the nicer neighborhoods in Richardson. Sivan started filling me in on how badly things were going at M-Gang. Amir didn't speak. He wouldn't even look at me. I couldn't tell if he was angry with me or if he was just upset in general. When we pulled into the Katzav's driveway, my jaw hit the floor.

To call this place a house would be understatement. The Katzavs lived in a friggen mansion!!! There was a huge living room-type area, two large dining rooms, and a "play room" where Sivan and Amir could work-out, play video games, watch TV, or generally do whatever they wanted. The walls were all mirrors, with a wooden bar going across one side like a ballet studio. I asked Sivan what it was.

"It's a dance bar. It's for ballet and jazz dance."

"You do that stuff?"

She hesitated, "Please don't tell anyone in the M-Gang.

They'll all think it's too . . . girly . . . for me, anyway. But I used to do ballet. It was my life before my aba died." She gestured over to a large portrait hanging on the other side of the doorway. Her father's picture looked scary. He was basically an older, even more muscular version of Amir. "That's why I was able to learn Krav so fast. You get a good enough body awareness and you can copy any move you see. If any of the Thorne Sveltes had committed more than one evening to learning Krav, you would have gotten to see this phenomena first-hand."

"So how long has it been since you danced?"

"About two days. I still do it all the time. I just hide it from the other M-Gangers." She smiled. "We all have our secrets. My mother had this room built when we moved into this house about two years ago. Zippy always thought this was just a good fight-training room. She never knew what I did in here when she wasn't staying over."

She spun around in a ballet-like move. "So what's your secret?"

Never in a million years did I ever think I'd admit this to anyone in the M-Gang, especially not Sivan, but here goes. "My uncle owns a small recording studio. I started writing songs when I was nine, and he lets me record them. I play the guitar a little. And I play the piano a little. I used to sing in various children's choirs. Then I started doing orchestra in sixth grade and I hated it. About the only instrument I was NEVER good at was the damned violin. And that's the only instrument my parents ever cared about."

"I'll have to hear one of your songs someday."

That thought scared me, "Um . . . if I'm on my deathbed."

She laughed, "It can't be that bad."

We headed over to Sivan's bedroom, which was miles different from Zippy's. Whereas Zippy had various rock-band posters plastered all over her walls, Sivan had a collection of dance-related paraphernalia. And by the way, this bedroom was enormous. There was an adult-sized bed, a mini-couch, and a full entertainment system, complete with a larger TV than my family owned. Where did the Katzav's come into this much money?

Sivan slouched across the mini-couch while Amir shut the door behind me. I sat on the edge of the bed while Amir just plopped down on the floor in the corner.

Amir started, "Okay sis, this was your idea. What's up???"

Sivan looked directly at me, "I think Dagan is getting played. I think we all are."

I sat for a second, thinking about that. No, it didn't make sense. "Sivan, nobody plays Zippy."

"Mark, I've known her for five years. She's not herself. I think I know why. Amir, tell him."

Amir looked at the ground, "I was pissed at you, Cohen. And I was sick of my sister sticking up for you. We got into a fight . . . she won. But . . ."

Sivan got sick of waiting, "He was pissed at you because of a bunch of garbage that Dr. Shadad had been telling him. He was in my face because Dr. Shadad had been telling him he was going to have to choose between his sister and the team. He told Shadad that I was making him stick by you, so Shadad spent a couple of sessions revving poor Amir up to get into a fight with me. And it worked."

I had a hard time swallowing this. "Amir, what did I ever do to you?" He just looked at the floor. I turned to Sivan, "Why would Dr. Shadad want to-"

Sivan interrupted, "Why did he tell Amir that you and I had made out back in Tel Aviv???"

"WHAT?!?!?" I know that Zippy made up something about me kissing Sivan as part of a cover story last summer, but Amir knew that this was a cover story, and . . . making out with Sivan?? What the hell?!?!?!

"Yeah. He told Amir that you admitted that we 'made

out' in Tel Aviv, and you ditched me for Tsipporah. He told Amir that I'd never 'admit' to it, but that it had happened and he needed to 'stick up' for his sister's honor since I wouldn't 'stick up' for myself."

"I never . . . that never . . . what the . . . you not sticking up for yourself . . . you would have torn my friggen throat out if I had . . ." I couldn't complete a sentence. This was insane.

"He tried to tell ME that you were coming unglued. He told ME that I should watch out for you because you might try to hurt some of the other M-Gangers. He tried to tell me that I might have to protect Amir from you."

Stunned. I had no words whatsoever. I started thinking about what he'd told me in our last couple of sessions: Zippy's just another teenage girl, she's cruel, she gets off on being mean to boys, she'll pretend to love me and then hurt me for her own amusement . . . and all the time HE was trying to turn Sivan and Amir into hating me?!?!?

"Why- Why would he do this?"

Sivan shook her head, "Does it matter? I don't know what he told Tsipporah, but I think he may have been poisoning her head somehow."

I thought for a minute, "So what do we do???"

"WE don't do a thing. YOU have to break her."

"How am I supposed to-"

"Just confront her!!! When she is hard to you, you need to confront her."

"But Sivan, that's what Shadad has been telling me that I should-"

"Not physically!!! You don't need to get into a fight. You just need to call her out and BE HONEST. You haven't done anything to her. I cannot believe she would fail to see that if you just confronted her with it. Mark, she obsessed over you for four years. She STALKED you for years. You are so much more than just another boy to her. Besides, I already told you that I will not fight your fights for you. I will support you when push comes to shove, but I will not fight FOR you if you will not fight for yourself."

Amir chimed in, "And it's all going to end pretty soon if someone doesn't confront her. I'm going to quit M-Gang if this doesn't stop. I didn't sign-up for THIS."

We all went into the living room to do Krav training. Training under Sivan was wholly different than training under Zippy. We did a structured run-through of every strike: 20 punches, 20 front kicks, 20 front elbows, etc. Then we did every self-defense technique at least three times, rotating partners every minute. Sivan would attack me, and vice versa. Then she'd attack Amir, then vice versa. Then Amir and I would go after each other. Then we spent an hour free-style sparring. We'd rotate partners every two minutes.

I never even noticed when Mrs. Katzav came through the door to watch us. She finally interrupted and joined in for a round or two to point out what each one of us could do differently to be more effective. This was one of the first times an adult had given me a Krav lesson. It was kinda scary, actually. Mrs. Katzav was like a cop. She was shouting the whole time, and moving faster than I could blink. She must have been one awesome assassin back when she worked for Mossad.

But despite the scariness, it was just plain fun working with these three people. Afterwards, Mrs. Katzav ordered pizzas and we all watched a movie in the play room.

The next morning, they all went off to their Synagogue for Shabbat service. They couldn't take me with them for fear that Zippy would see me and figure out about our little . . . rebellion. That afternoon when they came home, Amir and I played a basketball game against each other while Sivan danced in the playroom.

That evening, we trained again. Then I introduced them to Dark Shadows when it came on at 8. I loved that show, but they had a hard time understanding it. I was going to really love these weekends.

CHAPTER NINETEEN – BREAKING POINT

Friday, March 9th, 1991, 4:00pm

This morning I said goodbye to my parents for the next two weeks. Their flight to Hawaii was today, so when they dropped me off at school, that was going to be it until their return next week during Spring Break.

Of course, they didn't know it yet, but I was going to be on a "retreat" with the M-Gang kids throughout Spring Break, which was code for me staying with the Katzavs and training every night. At least that was the plan.

But when Mrs. Katzav picked me up from school this afternoon, she was alone. Apparently, the Dagans had taken Sivan and Amir for some special last minute training at M-Gang. The NSA guys thought they were close to tracking down Benson, so M-Gang needed to step up its preparations.

I didn't know what to do. Was I going to spend the entire evening with Mrs. Katzav? "Where are we going to go?" I asked.

"I'm taking you to M-Gang. That's where you belong, anyway."

"Yeah . . . some people don't think so."

"I know, Mark. Sivan told me that Dagan is getting . . . unpleasant with you."

Now there was a diplomatic word for the whole situation. "Yeah. She hates me."

"MARK!!! No. Tsipporah does not hate you. She loves you. She put up a huge fight to get everyone in M-Gang to accept you. You may not know this, but Sivan originally did not want you to be a part of M-Gang."

"I know. She used to not like me, but that was last year."

"Well . . . Sivan had her own demons to confront regarding you."

I had no idea what she meant by that, and she could tell from my expression that I was completely lost. So she changed the topic back to Zippy. "I understand Dagan does not allow you to train."

"No. She wants me out of M-Gang altogether."

"What?!?!? Since when???"

"Since that night that she and all the other M-Gangers drove off and left me and Sivan alone on the side of the road at midnight to fend for ourselves."

SCREEEEEEECH!!!!!! If I hadn't been wearing a seatbelt, it would have launched me through the window like a missile. I didn't know you could slam the breaks on a bullet van that hard.

"What?!?!?!?"

"Zippy, the Chaperones, the M-Gangers—they all got into cabs and left me and Sivan alone on the side of the road outside the safe-house in downtown Dallas. It was around midnight on some Saturday last month. And Zippy told me she wanted me out when Sivan and I made our way back to M-Gang."

"Don't make stories up, Mark. This is serious. If she

did something like that-"

"Zippy wasn't alone. It was everyone. That was the night Sivan put the last couple of chaperones in the emergency room. That's WHY she beat them up!!!"

"She never said anything about them abandoning you. She just said that she'd convinced the NSA guys that they were incompetent. Dammit. I should have known something was wrong. That was after she got into that horrible fight with Amir when . . . I had always told her to never hurt her brother because she would feel terrible if she did, but that day she fought him like she didn't care. I watched my poor son crying and holding an ice-pack on himself. I was so angry with her. Damn!!!! DAMN!!! I knew something was wrong. Tell me what happened that evening."

I told her everything: them keeping me in the cold for the fifth week in a row, them leaving me out there so that they could all go eat, Sivan sticking by my side, Sheri attacking me with a stun-gun, the entire team leaving me and Sivan alone, and finally Sivan capturing a bad guy by herself. Apparently, the NSA guys were keeping Sivan's mom COMPLETELY in the dark about M-Gang activities.

She was PISSED!!!

"I don't care what they do. I don't care if they shut down the entire program. That Sanders idiot is going to answer to me for all of this. And those damned chaperones."

"Sivan attacked them and put them both in the hospital that night. They're done."

She huffed, "They'd best thank whatever god they believe in that it was Sivan and not me. And what the hell was Dagan thinking?!?!? There's no way that her parents know about this. They'd put a stop to it if they did. Someone is pulling her strings if she's acting like that."

"Sivan think's it's our therapist."

"Your THERAPIST??? I thought the Americans didn't

want you seeing psychologists."

"No. They just didn't want us seeing Mossad psych guys. They hooked us up with an NSA shrink the day they took over. And he . . . he makes me uncomfortable. But Sivan thinks he's up to something because he's been telling her weird stuff."

"Like what?"

"Well, Sivan told me about her fight with Amir, and she said that Dr. Shadad had made Amir-"

She grabbed my lapel and yanked me forward, "What did you say his name was???"

"Dr. Shadad."

She looked like she'd seen a ghost. She slowly let go of me, "I'm sorry, Mark. I'm sorry. I shouldn't have reacted like that. Could you describe this 'Shadad' for me?"

I described him, and her face got darker with every word. She looked ready to explode by the time we started back down the road. She didn't say another word. She just drove. I hadn't been so scared for my life since . . . well since riding in a car on the streets of Tel Aviv. Israeli drivers are scary enough as it is. When one is pissed, let's just say you pray a lot and cling to anything you can grab onto.

We got to the Jewish Community Center. She didn't even bother trying to park the car. She just screeched it to a halt right in front of the building and stormed through the front door. I followed. Agent Williams was there and she was in his face within seconds.

"Where's your boss???"

"Ma'am, you're not supposed to get involved. Remember? Now why don't you just-"

She lashed out and grabbed him by the throat, "Let me make myself perfectly clear. Blood WILL be spilled tonight. It might be yours. Call him, NOW!!!" I guess it was her charming demeanor, but he did just that. She went over to the other phone and called the Dagans.

As much as I wanted to watch the show when Mrs. Katzav got her hands on Sanders, I felt drawn to the training room. I knew that I was not welcome there, but I knew that I had to go. Whatever the consequences, I had to end this "shut out in the cold" nonsense tonight. I was afraid of Zippy telling me to get out of M-Gang once and for all. I was afraid of all my other friends there doing the same. Deep down, I was also afraid of Sivan and Amir joining in, even though I should have known better. I put on my gear, and headed towards the training room.

When I arrived, they were doing a "man in the middle" drill. That's the Krav drill where one person defends himself while everyone else attacks. Amir was in the middle, and doing a pretty good job holding his own against the other six kids.

Zippy called a time-out the moment she noticed me.

"What are you doing here, Cohen? You can't be here."

Sheesh, nice to see you too. I had a few choice things I wanted to say, but I wasn't going to get anywhere by being overly aggressive. I was just going to stick to the truth— just like Sivan and I discussed. "I'm a member of this team, Zippy. I'm here to work out."

She paused for a minute. "You should turn right back around and leave, Cohen. You don't belong here."

"Zippy, what's your problem with me?"

She looked stunned, as though she couldn't believe someone was daring to challenge her. "Excuse me???"

"I said 'what's your problem with me.' What the hell did I ever do to you? We were best friends and now you're acting like-"

"I'm not going to argue with you, Cohen. I'm not talking about it. You're just going to-"

"Oh, that's good. You're not going to talk about it. You're just going to go on shutting me out of M-Gang. And who's next? Sivan? Aaron? Amir? Who are you going to turn on next? Do you even-"

"Shut up, Cohen!!! I'm tired of dealing with you."

"Seriously!!! What did I ever do to you??"

"Maybe I just got tired of 'oh poor me, the other kids at school beat me up and I don't have any friends and oh poor me.' Maybe I just got tired of being your damned bodyguard."

"Zippy, I can hold my own. You know that."

"You couldn't even fight off a bunch of middle-schoolers till we came around. And now I've grown sick of you and your attitude!!!" Aaron, Sheri, Rachael and Danny all nodded and chimed in their agreement.

"What the hell are you talking about??? What attitude-"

"This 'I'm better than everyone else' attitude you've got. I'm sick of it. You were nothing before I came around. You were nothing before these 7 kids took you in. And now we're sick of you acting like you're the best of us."

I didn't even know how to respond to this. It was like she was living in some other world. What was she talking about?? I didn't act like I was in charge of anything. "Zippy, who's feeding you this crap!!!"

"Nobody's feeding me anything. You're the one who's done the things you've done."

"WHAT THINGS have I done???"

"Stop acting like you don't know!!! Seriously, just leave. I don't want to talk to you about this anymore. This conversation is over."

I stood my ground. "The hell it is. Zippy, you know me better than anyone else. After all, you STALKED me for years."

She looked stunned, "Oh is THAT what you believe now? Figures!!! You also thought I was using you back in Tel Aviv!!! Using YOU!!! Hah!!! Like I'd ever NEED to use YOU for anything. You were absolutely worthless. And you still are!!!"

"I was worth enough to save your life at Dizengoff."

"Oh you want to discuss that, eh? You think bursting in

when Hassan let his guard down makes you a fighter? You think sucker punching that Bible teacher makes you a fighter? Where was all this 'fight' last year when you were crying on my shoulder?"

Why was she trying to hurt me again? And why weren't Sivan and Amir chiming in? I figured I'd do exactly what Sivan had suggested: be honest. "Zippy, I haven't done a damned thing to you. But if you're so pissed at me for whatever reason, if you want to hurt me, why don't you just come over here and take a shot at me like you want to? Huh? Why the backstabbing? Why the petty BS? Why all the talk?"

This was my final bluff. I was positive Zippy would never cross that line. She'd never physically hurt me. She was pretty far gone, but physical violence against someone who wasn't trying to hurt her was too much. I hoped.

"Thought you'd never ask." Zippy walked over to the sparring gear table. "You want it this way? Okay Mark. You wanna 'train' with us? You wanna be a 'fighter tough guy' type? Come on!!!" She motioned like she wanted to fight me. She put her bright blue gloves back on and strapped the Velcro tight. I heard Aaron go "yeah" like this was a moment he'd been waiting a long time for. Sheri blurted out, "Kick his ass, Zippy." I guess I was wrong about her not crossing that line. This was really going to happen.

I just stared at Zippy, "You're serious??? You really want to fight me???"

The look she shot back across the room gave me chills. "Want to? That's putting it mildly. Going to? That's more like it. Fight? No. Beat you unconscious? Absolutely!" She WAS serious. This was no good. I could never stand up to Zippy. It would be an absolute slaughter. And even if I could land a punch . . . I'd never want to punch Zippy, despite how cruel she'd been to me. The thought made me sick.

She stepped into her fighting stance about 5 feet away from me. "Hope you're ready to defend yourself," she muttered.

"I'm not going to hit you, Zipps."

"Then I'm going to REALLY hurt you!!! You'd be better off defending yourself. Maybe then I'll go a little easier on you." Her voice was starting to sound like that unnatural calm she'd get into just before attacking someone.

I thought for a second. Maybe if I let her blow off a little steam, it'll be just like sparring. I went over to the gear table, picked up a pair of gloves, laced them up, and took a stance.

"Zippy, whatever you think I've done, I just want you to know-"

"Shut up, Cohen. I'm through discussing this with you."

I had to make a split second decision. Do I launch in on her or do I wait for her to attack?

I just couldn't do it, dammit. Even if she outright killed me, I couldn't hit Zippy. I stepped backwards out of my fighting stance and deliberately dropped my guard. "Zippy, please, think about what you're-"

"Shut the hell up!!" she screamed as she burst towards me.

I did my best to prepare for one of her signature kicks, when BAM!!!!! A blue explosion slammed into my face, throwing my head back and knocking me into the wall. Zippy had burst in and nailed me with a direct punch to the nose. I stumbled forward from the wall, attempting to get into a defensive stance when I felt another jolt. Zippy scissored her forearms across the sides of my neck and pulled me into a murderous clinch. I had no defense. This was not good.

CHAPTER TWENTY – SHOWDOWN

BAM!!! Zippy's knee exploded up between my legs. Fortunately, I had a cup on. But it still hurt like hell. It also lifted me completely off the ground. By the time my feet hit the floor, her second knee was already coming in. BAM!!! This one went straight into my tummy, completely knocking the wind out of me. Looks like she learned her lesson from hitting my cup. I tried fighting her clinch, but every time I started to catch my balance, she'd spin me around before I could get my arms in position.

BAM!!! Another knee into my tummy. I couldn't breathe. She'd completely knocked all the wind out of me. I also couldn't tighten my tummy muscles to try to fight off the incoming strikes. BAM!!! Now the pain in my tummy was unbearable. I started to panic. My efforts to fight the clinch were getting more desperate, and sloppier with each passing moment. BAM!!! I was going to throw up any second now.

She spun me into the wall. I don't think she meant to, but she was so enraged that she forgot all about her surroundings. The jolt of my body hitting the wall knocked her clinch loose and sent my arms flailing. She grabbed my left arm and pinned it to her shoulder, then started punching me in the side, right under my ribcage. Each punch felt like she was stabbing me all the way to the heart. I finally puked.

"Dagan, he's had enough!!!" Sivan shouted with a disturbing urgency.

Zippy stopped hitting me long enough to let me finish puking, then she threw me to the ground, straddled me, and . . . BAM BAM BAM!!! Her punches were like bricks shooting into my face.

"Dagan, STOP you're killing him!!!"

BAM BAM BAM BAM BAM!!! Zippy was rapid-fire punching me in the face as hard as she could. It was like a machine gun. She must have hit me at least eight times per second. I couldn't even get my arms up to protect my face because the punches were coming so quickly.

"GET THE HELL OFF HIM!!!!"

Something jolted Zippy completely off of me. It took a few seconds for my eyes to focus—and for me to realize that Sivan had hooked her arm around Zippy's neck, pulled her off of me, and thrown her half-way across the room—all in one move.

"Have you gone insane??? He's your friend. You're friggen killing him!!!!!"

Zippy was panting. "I'm just getting started. Get out of my way, Katzav!!"

Sivan moved in between us and took a fighting stance.

Zippy was taken aback for a moment. "Are you serious? You're ready to fight me over MARK????"

Sivan nodded her head. "If you want to hurt him. You have to come through me."

Zippy let out a grin. "No too difficult . . . I taught you most of your skills anyway."

Zippy burst in on Sivan. Sivan blocked her incoming kick, simultaneously throwing a stomp kick into Zippy's stomach which sent them both back a few steps. I'd sparred Sivan many times. Her unnaturally long legs are like pistons when they shoot into you. I almost felt sorry for Zippy. But not for long.

Zippy burst in again, this time faking a kick and launching a punch right at Sivan's throat. Sivan deflected it, pulled Zippy in, threw two vicious knee-strikes into her stomach, and backed away before Zippy could recover.

I immediately realized what Sivan was doing. She was doing exactly what we'd taught at that "Lady's Self Defense" class. She was addressing the immediate danger and throwing simultaneous counterstrikes. She was overlapping her moves. Then she was getting the hell out of there—sting and run.

The third time it happened, Zippy started to catch on as well. "ENGAGE you coward!!!!!" she panted. Sivan had just deflected her attack, responded with a lightning-fast roundhouse kick to Zippy's ribs, and backed away before Zippy could recover.

Sivan just shook her head. "YOU want this fight. Not me. I will not let you hurt Mark. But I don't want to hurt you either. Tsippi, listen to me-"

Zippy burst in wildly at Sivan, this time throwing an outright reckless punch at her face. Sivan caught the punch with her forearms, then locked onto Zippy. Zippy immediately spun her right foot behind her so that Sivan wouldn't be able to throw a knee into her groin or tummy.

But Sivan had other plans. She threw a murderous knee right into the middle of Zippy's left thigh!!! It was the "boyfriend" move we'd taught after the "Lady's Self Defense" class. I remembered Sivan's advice to the drill-team girl: "Give him the most brutal dead-leg you can, and let it stand as a warning of how bad it's going to hurt if you fired that shot into his groin." It completely knocked Zippy backwards and she let out a scream!!!

Sivan didn't hesitate. She fired another devastating knee right into the same spot on Zippy's thigh, and Zippy crumpled to the ground. Sivan backed away as quickly as she could.

"Dagan, listen to me. Dr. Shadad has been lying to us. He tried to convince me that I'd need to hurt Mark to protect Amir. He's also been trying to turn Amir against me. He's been trying to turn me against both you and Mark. Tsippi, please!!!"

Zippy slowly forced herself up to her feet. She was crying from the pain. I'd been dead-legged a few times in school. The pain is unbearable. I couldn't imagine standing up after taking either of the shots Sivan had landed on her.

She tried to burst in on Sivan, but her left leg just couldn't do it and she stumbled. As soon as she caught her balance and planted her left foot on the floor, Sivan caught her with an explosive roundhouse kick. SMACK!!! Sivan's shin caught Zippy's left thigh right in the exact same dead-leg spot. If it had landed a few inches lower, it would have shattered Zippy's knee. She screamed again and crumpled.

"Tsippi, PLEASE!!! I can't stand hurting you!! Please don't make me do this anymore. I don't want to hurt you."

After a few seconds, Zippy forced herself back up on her feet. She couldn't put any weight on her left leg. WAS SHE COMPLETELY NUTS??? She looked almost like the boy in the Karate Kid movie at the very end, where he's fighting on one leg. She just stood there staring at Sivan, panting and trying not to show how much pain she was in. I think both girls were unsure of what to do next.

Sivan spoke up first, "Please listen to me. Whatever Shadad told you to make you hurt Mark—it was a lie."

"How could you know? What do you know about my meetings with Shadad?"

Sivan dropped her guard. After all, what could Zippy do? She typically kicked with her right leg, but that would require her to be able to stand on her left, which she couldn't do. She couldn't kick with her left because she could barely move it. She couldn't burst in on Sivan, and even if she tried, Sivan's unnaturally long legs would knock her into next week before Zippy could get close enough to do any damage. The fight was over.

The peaceful gesture was returned. Zippy dropped her hands as well.

Sivan pleaded, "Tsippi, I know you don't feel right about what you've been doing. I know you're letting your anger make your decisions for you. And when you're not angry anymore, you're going to be disgusted at the things you've done. Look!!!" She pointed over at me, "Tsippi, this is MARK you're hurting!!! He'd do anything for you. He saved your life at Dizengoff. LOOK AT HIM!!! Look what you did to him!!!"

She looked over at me. She must have done some serious damage to me because when she looked over, her face changed. Zippy just stood there for a minute—still panting—but her breathing was beginning to slow down. She looked back at Sivan.

Sivan's voice began to soften, "Tsippi, this is that 'little boy' you wanted to protect for all those years—the one you said pulled you out of the darkness. This is the same boy who all those kids made up lies about. This is the same boy who all those people hurt because of lies they believed about him. You wanted to beat the hell out of all those people last year. But now you're hurting him because Shadad has told you lies about him. You've become those people. Tsippi . . . look at what you've done."

Zippy looked over at me and started to cry again, but this time it didn't look like it was from the pain shooting through her leg, and she let out this horrible sounding scream. Sivan just stood there, not sure whether to comfort Zippy or keep her safe distance. Zippy fell to her knees, sobbing uncontrollably.

The door burst open and Mrs. Katzav came running in. She took one look at me, then took one look at Zippy. She started babbling at Sivan in Hebrew. Sivan did plenty of babbling back. Then they collected Zippy and left the room. On her way out, Mrs. Katzav shouted at Amir, "Take care of him."

The rest of the M-Gangers just stood there. Amir came over and started tending to me. Apparently, my face was starting to swell and I looked like I'd taken a few thousand bee stings. Sheri, Rachael and Danny just stood there staring.

Amir got me to my feet just and we headed over to the lounge. He put ice packs on my face and side. Then he called 911. Before he could start making up a story, Agent Williams showed up and took over the call. Here comes another damned ambulance.

Saturday, March 10, 1991, 3:00 am

The worst part of going to the emergency room when you're underage is that they WILL NOT even look at you without a parent present. You just sit there. It doesn't matter how broken or close to death you are, they won't do so much as one single X-Ray without parental consent. Which doesn't really work out well when your parents are in Hawaii.

The worst part of showing up at the emergency room all beaten-up when you're underage is that they call the police and Child Protective Services. They have to, by law.

That is, unless, you show up in the "custody" of a federal agent. When that happens, they see you right away. They don't summon the police. They don't call CPS. They don't even call your parents.

So I immediately got a bunch of X-Rays, an MRI, and a bunch of other medical-science stuff I really have no hope of understanding. The short version was this: two broken ribs, a concussion, and several "contusions" which are like bruises, only a thousand times worse. I've got contusions on my liver and all over my face. I also had a broken nose.

They patched my nose and put a bunch of padded junk all over the ribs. They gave me some "painkillers" that didn't really make anything stop hurting, but made my dizzy as hell. And they told me to "take it easy" for a few weeks.

Then we were out of there. Wow that was fast. I'd been to the hospital several times when Elise got sick. We'd never even got to see a doctor this quickly. This time we were in and out in under two hours. Amazing.

I dozed off on the way back to M-Gang headquarters. That stuff they gave me really had my head spinning. Williams woke me up when we got back to the Jewish Community Center. When we went through the lobby, the other kids couldn't stop staring at me. My face must have been banged up pretty badly.

We stopped outside the room where Zippy, Sivan, Agent Sanders, Zippy's parents, and Sivan's mom were all arguing. I could see through the door that Zippy was sitting on a table. Sivan was pressing an ice-pack on Zippy's thigh and trying to comfort her.

Zippy's mom was shouting at Sanders, "This is NOT how you handle agents, to say nothing of children. You do NOT put them with some shrink and give him license to say whatever to the kids. You do NOT leave them unattended with each other, especially when you start noticing problems."

"Mrs. Dagan, please-"

"No!!! We've spent the last three years building this program. We've build this team. We've built these kids into damned good agents. And you've torn it apart in a matter of months. You've got the other children shunning Cohen—a child who's been shunned so much in his life that it's a miracle he ever even SPEAKS to children his own age. You've got Amir and Sivan getting into an actual physical fight with each other. Then you pull a REAL miracle out of your hat and get MY LITTLE TSIPPORAH to attack Cohen!!!"

"Ma'am, they're children. They will occasionally get a little rough."

"A little rough?!?!? Sivan says that if she hadn't pulled my Tsipporah off of Cohen, she'd have killed him!!! You call that a little rough???"

"Ma'am, she's probably being a little dramatic. I doubt she'd have really killed-"

Mrs. Katzav interrupted, "She was not. I saw what was left of Cohen after Tsipporah finished with him."

Zippy tried to chime in, "Imeh-"

"Not another word, Tsipporah Liraz!!! I didn't teach you to wield violence so that you could hurt your friends." Okay, Zippy's mom was pissed.

Agent Williams motioned for me to follow him. He went ahead and walked through the door and announced, "Cohen's here." I started to follow him.

Mr. Dagan got up, "Ahhh let's have a look at this- MY!!! GOD!!!" The utter horror on his face confirmed YET AGAIN that I didn't want to look in a mirror. Mrs. Dagan and Mrs. Katzav both gasped at the same time. They were slowly approaching me like they were afraid I'd break if they moved too quickly.

Mrs. Dagan put her hand on my cheek while examining my face. She whispered out "Dear God, Tsipporah, what did you do?!?!?!"

Zippy glanced at me for a second, then looked at the ground. She couldn't stand to view her work.

Mr. Dagan sat calmly and asked his daughter, "Tsipporah, what could this head-shrinker possibly say to you that would get you to do . . . this? You already knew about him shooting Hassan unarmed. You already knew Mark wasn't the best fighter, but he was improving. You two were like siblings last summer. What could POSSIBLY change you so much that you . . . LOOK at him . . ." Mr. Dagan looked and sounded disgusted.

Zippy looked up at me for a second then looked back at

the ground, "It started out like . . . he told me I needed to 'distance myself' from Mark. He said it wasn't okay for kids our age to feel . . . you know. Then he said that Mark . . . admitted that . . ." she looked up at me, "that you told him you liked to . . . you know . . . touch yourself while looking at a picture of ME!"

WHAT?!?!? Do I even OWN a picture of Zippy? We're not exactly picture taking types. And by the way, WHAT THE HELL?!?!?

I had about a million thoughts go through my head in that moment, but one seemed to rise to the forefront of my mind: here we go again. Last year, a lot of people really hurt me because someone told them a lie about me—a lie involving sex-stuff. And now this year, all the hurt and all of Zippy's meanness because someone made up yet another damned sex-stuff lie about me. Again, WHAT THE HELL?!?!?

Mrs. Dagan was the first to respond, "And you believed this?"

Zippy nodded. I'd never had much luck denying the sex-stuff lies people made about me, but I figured I'd give it one last try here, "Zippy, I never-"

"Quiet, Cohen. You should not be trying to speak right now." Mrs. Dagan cut me off, "I'm not concerned about this shrink's stories, anyway. I'm concerned that my daughter, whom I TRAINED to think smarter than this, fell for something so obviously and outrageously false and calculated to disgust and manipulate her!!! I'm concerned that my daughter could be so easily misled!!!"

Okay, at least ONE person didn't just knee-jerk believe sex-stuff about me.

Zippy just looked at the ground. "Then he started talking about how it was murder for Mark to kill Hassan because he was no longer a threat . . . and how I was just as bad for not stopping him. And I was dirty and Mark was making me dirty by . . . you know. And I started having bad dreams about Mark and . . . I don't know why I just . . . I . . ." she started sobbing again.

"Tsipporah, look at me."

Zippy just kept looking down, ashamed and sobbing uncontrollably.

"LOOK AT ME, TSIPPORAH LIRAZ!!!" Mrs. Dagan could be scary when she was pissed.

Zippy looked up at her mother.

"First, post-combat trauma psychologists don't usually go into someone's sex life. At least in Israel they don't. So there would be no reason for Mark and your doctor to discuss this. Is this normal for Americans?" She looked back at Sanders.

The buttoned-up agent responded, "Well ma'am, we don't usually send folks to see psychologists after their first kill. We usually just give them a bottle of whiskey, and that takes care of any 'trauma' problems right away."

She stared back at him with complete disgust. "Shocking," she uttered with a mix of condescension and sarcasm.

Sanders continued, "Well, it's not like we tried to give the kids whiskey or anything. This was something new—trying to give them a therapist."

Mrs. Dagan simply sighed and turned back to Zippy, "This was your first experience with one, so I cannot expect you to know this. You're off the hook for that one. But you should know that no psychologist would ever tell YOU something that ANOTHER PATIENT had confided in him, even if it were true. That should have raised a red flag for you."

Zippy looked at the ground and started to sob again. She'd been suckered. She'd been used as a patsy. She'd hurt me, and it was starting to all hit her at once.

Mrs. Dagan turned back to Sanders, who responded "That's true, ma'am. If a psychologist breaks confidence, he loses his license. He's finished as a doctor."

Sivan's mom piped up, "I told you we couldn't trust this guy. Sivan and Amir have been getting so distant from the others. And Cohen . . . and now we know that it's Shadad of all people."

"Miriam, it might not be Chaim. It might be a different Shadad. We don't know yet. We can't go jumping to conclusions and-"

"LOOK AT COHEN!!! Look at little Tsippi!!! Who else but Chaim Shadad??? And where has he been all this time?"

Agent Sanders interrupted, "Dr. Shadad has worked with us for years. He's one of the best profilers we've got. And he's a good guy. When I asked if he knew anyone who could be the therapist for this group, he volunteered himself immediately."

The other three adults looked at him like he was crazy. Sivan's mom finally spoke up, "And that didn't raise any suspicions at all? A profiler agreeing to be the therapist for a bunch of kids who'd just seen military-style combat."

Sanders reached up and scratched his head for a second, "That should have jumped out at me. You're right. There should have been red flags with him. He told the kids to not talk about therapy with their parents. That was weird. The kids all seemed to get worse the more they talked to him. And now we know he was telling them things that were WAY outside of normal parameters."

Sivan's mom seemed to relax a bit, "So can we all finally agree that this psychologist needs to be brought in for questioning?"

"I want to kill him," Zippy muttered.

"No." Mrs. Dagan looked like she was like she was being forced to admit something unwillingly, "If he's working to derail M-Gang, there are a limited number of people who he could be working for—one of them is this Benson guy. If there's a chance we can get any information from him . . ."

Robert Linus Koehl

"I'm with your daughter on this one, Hadassah. We need to terminate him, and I don't mean that we send the children to do it. We used to be a team—the three of us and Shlomo. WE were the four-person assassination team, not our children," Sivan's mom said with an air of nostalgia in her voice.

Sivan spoke up, "Can't we do both? Interrogate him until we've got everything we need, then terminate him."

Everyone looked around like what she'd said was just too obvious. It was agreed. But Sanders pointed out that the three adults hadn't been mission ready in some time. The kids were going to have to make the capture. The adults started planning. I dozed off again on the recliner in the lobby—damned hydrocodone.

CHAPTER TWENTY-ONE –
REVELATION

Saturday, March 10, 1991, 11:00 a.m.

"Mark . . . Mark, time to get up." It was Zippy. I realized the room had been emptied of people. It was just me, Zippy, and Sivan. And the sun was up.

Sivan was standing a few feet away. Zippy had her hand on my shoulder.

"How long have I been out?" I was trying to shake this overbearing grogginess. I officially *HATE* hydrocodone. I don't know how bad these bruised organs and broken ribs are going to hurt, but it's going to have to get pretty bad before I take another one of these things.

Sivan answered, "It's lunch time. We went to Campari's and got you a minestrone, that lemon artichoke pasta, and that cake you like so much. Tsippi said they were your favorites."

That put a smile on my face, which kinda hurt. I could feel how swollen my face still was.

Zippy put her arms around me and hugged me tightly,

"I'm so SO sorry, Mark. I WILL!!! MAKE!!! THIS!!! RIGHT!!! I swear it!!"

Sivan smiled at the sight.

When Zippy pulled away, tears were streaming down her cheeks. She looked back at Sivan, "Do you want to tell him, or shall I?"

Sivan gestured for Zippy to tell me, so she did. "Sivan called Shadad's pager and left a 911 message. When he called back, he claimed to be in Colorado on emergency business. But Agent Sanders traced the call. He's staying at some ritzy hotel in downtown Ft. Worth. We're leaving at three and breaching his hotel room at 6. Sivan planned the whole mission. All eight M-Gang kids will enter at once. There will be no more of this nonsense where he gets one or two of us alone and turns us on each other. My parents and Sivan's mom will be in the hotel lobby. The American agents will be waiting behind at M-Gang headquarters."

Sivan interrupted, "There's just one snag. The adults want us to take him alive. We've only been authorized to use deadly force if he resists."

Then both girls looked at each other, then looked at me and said in unison, "So we need to make sure he resists." Both of them burst out giggling. It was a welcome sight. The two of them had been like siblings last summer in Israel, constantly laughing together. I'd missed this sight for a while.

Sivan looked over at me, "Any ideas on how to do that?"

I shrugged, "Depends on your definition of resistance. I personally think you just need to tell him to 'shut up' and see how long it takes for him to start babbling again."

Both girls chuckled. Sivan nodded in agreement, "Yes. That's the best thing about today's mission. I don't have to listen to his endless babble in those damned therapy sessions anymore."

With that, Zippy handed me the "to go" bag from

Campari's. "So you best eat now. We won't be having dinner till after the mission. Although I understand there's a great place in Sundance Square where we can get steaks tonight."

Sivan threw me the bottle of pills. "Take one with your lunch."

"Sivan, I really hate this stuff," I protested.

"Not as much as you're going to hate life when those ribs start screaming at you." She stopped. Zippy was looking at the ground. She was still really upset with herself and hearing Sivan talk about my injuries probably didn't help. Sivan continued, "If you take your pills now, the grogginess will wear off right as we get to Fort Worth. Then you can help us . . . make Shadad resist." She smiled.

I didn't argue.

Saturday, March 10, 1991, 6:00 p.m.

When you live in the Dallas suburbs, there are two things you know about Fort Worth. First, there is a big metropolitan city about an hour west of Dallas, called "Fort Worth." Second, it is wholly irrelevant to your life. Fort Worth is what people outside of Texas think all of Texas is like. People wear cowboy hats. People wear cowboy boots. People talk with country accents. There's a "rodeo," which I'm happy to say I've never attended. It's very much the cliché that all non-Texans think of when they think "Texan."

I hate those clichés. I haven't owned a pair of cowboy boots since I was five. I haven't worn a cowboy hat since I've been old enough to talk.

But my visits to Fort Worth so far have been generally happy. There's a futuristic site called "The Water Gardens," where some famous sci-fi films have been made. And tonight, we were going to be one block away from The Water Gardens—at one of the ritziest hotels in the entire area.

We drove to the site in two vans. I slept the entire way. Zippy and Sivan woke me up just as we were entering the downtown area. Our van pulled up to the hotel, and a bell boy guided us inside. We looked like a tour group, and the NSA guys had pre-booked a couple of rooms for us. Sivan's mom and Zippy's parents went to the front desk to get their keys. We waited.

After a few minutes, Sivan's mom handed Zippy a key and walked away. Zippy and Sivan motioned for all of us to head over to the elevators. Once all eight M-Gang kids managed to cram ourselves into an elevator, Zippy told us the plan. "The NSA arranged us a key to the room where we traced Shadad's call. He's in the Presidential Suite. It's a multi-room suite. There's a foyer where we can enter undetected. Once grouped in there, we clear the entire room in standard pattern. Everyone remember how to do that?"

We all nodded our heads yes. The elevator bell dinged. We all filed off, and drew our weapons.

Zippy pulled me aside, "You're with me. The last time we did a mission in hotel, it didn't work out so well for you. No?"

I heard Sivan over my shoulder, laughing at that. "I don't think there are any hot Arabic female ninja terrorists for him to go flinging himself at, Dagan. Not this time, anyway."

Okay, laugh it up, girls. I definitely had this coming.

"Well, if there are, Agent Sanders really needs to work on his intel capabilities," Zippy responded.

We got to the door and everyone hushed. Zippy leaned in and whispered to me, "Mark, are you okay to do this?"

"I'm ready."

"I know, but are you feeling any effects from the painkillers? I don't want you getting hurt again. If you're still feeling sluggish, tell me now."

I thought for a second, "I'm good."

Sivan whispered from behind me, "Are your ribs hurting?"

I sighed, "Yes, but not enough to affect me in there." I looked back at her, then looked forward at Zippy. "I'm good. Let's go get this guy."

Zippy looked at me for a long couple of seconds as though she was trying to find some reason to call the whole thing off. But not finding that reason, she fell into her unnatural pre-battle calm and whispered, "Okay, let's do this."

Sivan, Amir, and I crouched down on one side. Rachael, Sheri, Danny, and Aaron went to the other. Zippy positioned herself right in front of Sivan, just next to the door. She slowly put the key into the reader. It made a slight clicking sound and turned green. She turned the doorknob and opened the door just a millimeter.

We heard Shadad's voice. He was talking to someone. He thankfully hadn't heard the door open. Zippy got it cracked just enough to visually ensure that the upper latch wasn't locked, then she opened it the rest of the way. Shadad was well funded, but he wasn't an agent. In fact, he was a bit careless.

He was also talking VERY loudly.

Zippy, Amir, and I all crept into the foyer. Zippy looked around the corner to determine whether she could see Shadad. She looked back at us and shook her head no. There was a kitchen area dead ahead. Zippy made a silent sprint over towards it. Looking back, she motioned for Sivan, Amir, and me to follow her. We copied her silent spring and snuck over to the kitchen area.

The other four M-Gangers entered the foyer behind us. Rachel closed the door as silently as possible. She also locked the mechanical latch so that nobody could enter or exit without undoing it. We were at the point of no return. There was no exiting without Shadad finding out now. We were going all the way.

His voice got louder. He was in the living room, right around the corner from us. The four kids in the foyer clung to the wall to keep from being noticed.

The four of us in the kitchen crouched down.

Zippy crept forward, got a quick glance around the corner, and slipped back. She made a hand gesture to show us the he was on the phone, then put her finger up to her lips so that we'd be quiet. She turned and made the same gestures to the kids in the foyer. Danny made a thumbs-up signal to show that he understood. Shadad was outlining his grand plan to somebody on the other end of the line.

"No no, don't worry that, I've already neutralized them. They just don't know it yet . . . what? . . . No, not this time. None of us have to get our hands dirty. There's going to be a bloodbath. Several kids are going to be dead. It's going to make the news, and the Zionists won't be able to hide their crimes any more . . . when the people find out about this 'M Gang,' they'll have the image of several dead kids to show how great a program it is . . ."

Even though we had the drop on him and he had no way of knowing it, I still got chills hearing someone talk about killing me. He let out a chuckle, "No. That's the best part. One of the children in the M-Gang program is going to do it for us."

What?!?!?

"It's a plan as simple and as old as any ever attempted. Pick the most vulnerable subject, make the others turn on him, make him feel isolated, alone, and hurt, then just keep pouring it on until he snaps. Of course, it also helps to make suggestions to him . . . oh, it's the Cohen kid."

A boiling rage exploded down in my tummy. I already knew what this guy had done to me. But hearing him brag about it like that, I really wanted to shoot this guy.

"Yeah. It wasn't hard at all. The Dagan kid is the leader of the bunch. All I had to do was flip her, and she took all the others with her . . . yeah, the same, she and the Cohen kid were the ones who killed Shamil Hasan . . . what? . . . oh, yeah, definitely . . . no, it was easy. She was suffering PTSD from their operation in Tel Aviv. Making her blame him was nothing. No challenge at all. I almost felt cheated, it was so simple. It was the same three-step process I used on all the other kids. Detach, demonize, and mislead. Detaching her was the hard part. The rest was easy."

He started to chuckle, "Oh, how'd I do it? You want all my secrets, eh? Well, I convinced her that she'd be useless taking care of others if she didn't take care of herself first. It's true, but if you spin it just right, you can make someone stop taking care of those who need help. When she started seeing Cohen as helpless and overly-dependent on her, she detached. Then demonizing Cohen was easy. First, I made her feel disgusted at him. Then I just took her nightmares and put his face on them. She had some bizarre attachment to him, like he was a symbol of purity to her. I just had to make him impure in her eyes, and let her nightmares do the rest. She blamed him. She hated him. And she took the entire team with her."

Zippy and Sivan looked furious. Zippy backed up and pulled me and Amir into a huddle. "Wait until he's off the phone. We don't want to tip-off whoever is on the other end." We nodded and kept listening to Shadad's rant.

He was starting to get loud, "Oh it was beautiful!!! She absolutely broke him. That kid was in tears every time I saw him."

I felt Zippy's arm wrap itself around me. She looked at me with a terrible sadness in her eyes, and pulled me into a hug. She whispered in my ear "I'm so sorry, Mark."

". . . any day now. He's ready to snap. He'll probably take out Dagan and a few of the others. And the Katzav girl will take him out. She doesn't really go along with the others. She's completely detached. I was originally going to work on her, but she's nowhere near as damaged as the

Cohen kid. She's completely cold. She'll kill him without a second thought."

"Like hell," Sivan whispered. She and Zippy both crept up to the corner and made a hand signal to the kids in the foyer.

"What if they find out? Oh that's the beauty of it. Cohen's life was turned upside-down by sexual allegations last year. When he finds out the exact same thing is what's hurting him now, he'll snap. So it's a no-lose scenario. Either way, it'll be a bloodbath."

He laughed like he was entirely impressed with himself.

"Yes. Just sit back and watch. I just got off the phone with one of the kids this evening. It's going to happen really soon. When it's all over, the governments will be in disarray and you can safely leave the country . . . that's right . . . okay, I'll call you when it's done."

He hung up the phone and turned around to face seven Beretta 22s . . . and one Walther P-88.

CHAPTER TWENTY-TWO – CAUGHT IN THE ACT

"So that's what it was all about—all your talk about Mark being weak, all your talk about taking care of myself, all your talk about Mark being 'dirty,' all your talk about me being dirty, all your talk about me being tainted, all your talk about Mark being my 'failed redemption,' all your lies . . . this is what it was about!!!" Zippy was shaking with anger.

"Listen, Dagan-"

"Shut!!! The Hell!!! Up!!! I've heard quite enough from you. I listened to all of your 'you need to distance yourself from Mark Cohen' crap. I listened to all of your lies about Mark—the same damned lies other people used to hurt him last year!!! I listened to all your crap. I can't BELIEVE I didn't just shoot you last fall!!!"

"Dagan, I was just following orders. You've gotta believe-"

"Orders?!?!?! You're a fellow Jew. How many times was that line used at Nuremburg?" Did she really want to argue history with the guy?

"Tsipporah, it wasn't personal. It was just-"

"It was just me sharing every fear I ever had with you, every feeling I had about Mark and my friends. And it was you TWISTING that and making me hate Mark. I look back over the last year and I'm ASHAMED of myself. I'm ashamed of what I've done to Mark. I'm ashamed of the cruelty I've shown him. And you made me do it all."

"Oh me??? Tsipporah, I've only tried to get you to take responsibility for your actions. Something you still refuse to do. You were mean to poor Cohen. Big deal. Every girl your age is mean. Cohen should toughen up a bit and-"

Zippy interrupted, "-are you TRYING to make me shoot you? Because you no need to try so hard. I PLAN to shoot you. I just want to get a few things off my chest first. You hurt Mark through me. You wanted to make me hurt him so much that he would snap and kill me. Well, look at him. LOOK AT HIM!!!"

He obeyed.

She continued, "See how much I hurt him. I didn't just make him 'feel' alone, I didn't just leave him out to dry, and I didn't just abandon him mid-mission. I ATTACKED him last night because I listened to YOU!!! Well, now there's nothing you can say to save your wretched life because I am through listening. You made me really hurt someone who is most precious to me."

For the first time since I'd known him, the doctor had nothing to say.

"Worse," she looked around at each of the M-Gang kids, "we're Mark's family. He's our brother. And you got every person in this room except for Sivan to hurt him. He will never fully trust any of us again. And I no can blame him. No matter what we do to re-earn his trust, there will always be this little broken piece in the back of his mind— this little memory of us turning our backs on him—this little memory of us hurting him. And it will always hurt. And I can never take that hurt away!!! Everyone he knew betrayed him last year, but he always knew he could count on us, and . . . and then we . . . and then I took that away from him. And it was all because of YOU!!! You made us break him. Your damned lies-"

Sheri interrupted, "You told me I had to choose between Zippy and Mark!!! You told me that I couldn't trust Mark!!! You told me he was the reason why I had my big fight with Danny. You told me he had told Danny to see other girls and cheat on me. You told me he nearly got Danny to do it!!! Do you have any idea what I did to Mark??? I really hurt him last month. I attacked him while we were on a mission and I hurt him and I . . ." she started to cry, "I can't take it back. I can't change it." Danny put his arm around her.

Rachael joined in, "You told me he and Zippy were lying about getting Hassan—that Zippy had actually done it but Mark was taking credit. You told me that he had done terrible things and the adults were covering for him because he was their 'golden boy' and they'd protect him. You told me the adults would leave us all out to dry to protect him!!! You said they were already preparing to frame Danny for some of Mark's screw-ups. You said he was a glory hound, and that he'd get credit for anything I did."

Danny piped up, "You told me he was after Sheri. You said he was trying to steal her away from me."

Aaron just looked at the ground, "You said Mark stole my position on all those missions last summer. You said that Zippy used to like me but tossed me aside when Mark came onboard. You said that I should try to buddy up to her and make Mark look bad every chance I get. You said they both thought he was better than me." Zippy looked like she had been punched in the stomach.

We all looked at Amir, who said "I won't even repeat the crap you told me. To be honest, I don't even remember much of it because I wasn't paying attention. My sister saw right through you. She warned me not to trust you. She said you rubbed her the wrong way from the first meeting."

He looked over at Sivan. They smiled at each other. "She never put up with people hurting Mark. And she wouldn't put up with me doing it either, no matter how hard I tried to go along with Tsipporah."

Amir looked over at Zippy, "She said you'd lost your mind, not that I ever thought you were all there to begin with." He looked over at the others, "and that the rest of you had gone over the edge with Dagan." He looked over at me, "You know that Sivan and I were ready to quit the next time someone was cruel to you." Then he looked at Shadad, "You nearly won."

"Li- Listen, kids"

"Shut the hell up!" Zippy pointed her gun at his face so rapidly I honestly thought she was about to kill him. "Amir?"

He answered "Yes."

"Amir, please go and get your mom. Take Aaron with you. Rachael?"

"Yeah." She sounded so military.

"Take Danny and Sheri. Go get my parents. Tell them there's a dead body in this room, and they need to bring the cleaning kit." The sound of those words seemed to make Dr. Shadad shudder. But he was trying to keep on his best poker face. I'm sure he thought he could talk his way out of this situation.

"What about Mark?" Rachael asked.

Zippy gave an evil smile, "Mark deserves to see what I do to people who trick me into hurting him."

"What about Sivan?"

Zippy started to look aggravated, "Sivan stood by him. She even fought me to protect him. She deserves to see this too."

Rachael and Danny started for the door, but Sheri didn't budge. This annoyed Zippy, "Azel, go with the Steins and get my parents!!!"

Sheri stood there, tears still streaming down her face,

"Tsippi, I . . ."

Zippy sighed and relaxed a bit, "I know Sheri. I was there. I know what you did to Cohen. But I did worse."

"But Tsippi, I . . . I was so angry I would have killed him if Sivan hadn't stopped me."

"And that separates us how? You used a weapon. I used my hands. But I betrayed Mark much worse than you could have ever dreamed of. That's why I have to be the one to do this."

Sheri glanced over at me, still crying. She mouthed the words "I'm sorry" and joined Rachael and Danny. They all three walked out the door. With that, it was just me, Zippy, Sivan, and Dr. Shadad. Zippy just stood there for a few minutes. Shadad finally spoke, "Tsipporah, please let me explain-"

"There's nothing you can say. I'm just trying to decide how to kill you. Part of me wants to torture you for a while. Part of me wants to castrate you with a garlic-mincer just to see how long it takes for you to bleed to death. But part of me just wants to put a bullet in your head and be done with you. So please, don't offer me explanations, it interrupts my train of thought."

"Tsipporah, you don't need-"

"I can't BELIEVE how many different ways I want to kill you!!! It's so hard to pick just one. I'll tell you what." She put her gun down and walked over to Sivan. "You liked talking about darkness, I'll show you darkness. Sivan, do you have the dice I asked you to pack?"

"Right here, Dagan."

"Do you have the First Aid kit?"

"In my bag."

"Good. Dr. Shadad, you compared Mark to Haman in a couple of our sessions. You compared him to friggen HAMAN, the most evil anti-Semite in history. So I think it's only fair that we adopt a page from his book in dispatching you. Since I can't seem to decide how many different ways I want to kill you, we'll let fate decide." She took the dice from Sivan. "Just like Haman, I'll roll a pair of dice, and that'll be the number of times we revive you after you flat-line. Sivan, you think you can revive this guy after I kill him?"

"As long as it means I get to watch him die more than once tonight, I'll do anything to wake him back up."

"Good." She threw the dice on the floor. "Seven. Okay, let's have some fun."

She pulled out a stun-gun, "Shabak did a report where if you stick one of these over someone's heart, and zap them long enough, they'll have a heart-attack and die." She looked at me for a second, then shook her head, "No. That'll have to wait." Then she pulled out a little black pouch. After thinking for a second, she put it back in, "saving that one for Benson."

After digging around in her backpack for a few more seconds, she pulled out a mace can. "I read another Shabak report that said if you empty one of these directly into someone's mouth while holding their nose shut, it'll cause full respiratory arrest. You can watch them suffocate and convulse to death. That seems a good start to the evening. No? I can even spray some in his eyes and nose to maximize his suffering."

Sivan smiled and nodded her head at Zippy, "Much better, Dagan."

Zippy quickly walked towards him, shaking-up the mace can, "Open up, Doctor."

He started to back away from her. At that very moment, we heard the sound of a gun cocking from the doorway.

CHAPTER TWENTY-THREE – THE TERMINAL CHATTERBOX

"Chaim Shadad . . . I've been waiting years for this moment." It was Sivan's mom. She was standing at the door, pointing a small Beretta directly at his chest.

He just stood there.

"No hello, Chaim?"

"Hell- Hello Miriam."

She smiled, "Have a seat, Chaim."

He complied, falling back on the ugly grey couch.

"That's a good boy. You're good at taking orders. Aren't you, Chaim?"

"Mi- Miriam, you've gotta know-"

"I've!!! Got!!! To!!! Know!!! Only one thing: Where is the Hadawi girl?"

"I don't know any Hadawi-"

BANG!!!

The couch exploded between his legs. Sivan's mom had shot the couch about two inches below Dr. Shadad's privates. She very calmly raised the gun, and pointed it right at his groin. He got the message.

"I'll tell you everything!!!"

Mrs. Katzav looked unimpressed. "I know you will. But then again, what could you possibly tell us that's worth your life after what you've done? You'll probably just lie about the Hadawi girl's location anyway, and tell us a bunch of general low grade crap—probably stuff we knew already. Right, Chaim? You're good at that—telling us low grade crap we already know. Aren't you, Chaim?"

His eyes pled with her, but his mouth just ran off and said, "She's Palestinian, you know. The little girl is-"

Zippy spoke up at this point, "Palestinians are no our enemies. The killers among them are." She looked over at Sivan. The two of them exchanged a smile.

"That's right," Mrs. Katzav continued, "we aren't such blunt instruments that we cannot distinguish innocent from evil." Her face darkened, "And you made your choice long ago, didn't you Chaim?" She motioned like she was about to shoot him.

He panicked and shouted, "Listen, I know what they're planning!!!"

"Do you? Savak ransom teams just happen to spill their detailed plans to lackeys they paid off for information these days?" She sounded even more unimpressed.

"I helped with their plan."

"Oh, so they're inviting lackeys to help them plan now?"

"No! It's . . . it's a very long story."

"Then you should speak with haste because I've been waiting for this moment for years. I've been dreaming of shooting you in the groin and watching you bleed to death, or maybe slowly slashing you apart with a thousand individually non-lethal cuts, or slowly melting your body inch by inch with acid. I've killed many men, but you would be the only one I'd ever taken my time with, Chaim. Speak quickly before my self-restraint fails me, and this better be good." She sounded almost robotic.

"Six years ago, a man named Shamil Hassan contacted

me." We all shuddered at the sound of his name. "He had brokered a deal between some resistance fighters in the West Bank-"

"TERRORISTS, Mr. Shadad. Call them what they are if you intend to live."

"Okay," he held up his hands "terrorists in the West Bank. It was a deal between them and some rather wealthy interests in Iran. Anyway, they had learned of some American technology firms which were working on new high-tech weapons for the American government."

"I know this already. You planned to kidnap the children of several key designers, and use them to get information on the latest American weapons. My husband and I were on the Mossad team assigned to protect them. Or have you forgotten?"

He was really starting to shake. Sivan's mom knew a lot more than she'd ever let on. And he knew she knew it. And it scared the hell out of him. He continued, "Hassan contacted me in April of 1986. He informed me that the extraction would be impossible because Mossad was guarding the target's family. But the Mossad agents had gotten careless. They were here with their families. So we targeted their children for ransoming. I helped with the plan."

"I KNOW THAT, Chaim!!! We trusted you!!! You were ex-Mossad. You were a Jew. You were even Sephardic for God's sake. We TRUSTED YOU!!!" I'd never heard Sivan's mom shout like this. "And you sold out our family's location to Savak!!!"

Did I hear her correctly? Dr. Shadad was the one who told the Savak wet-team where to find Sivan's family—and Zippy's family???

"I know. Yes. Please. Please let me . . . Hassan gave me operational control of the teams on the ground back then. I had all the details. It's the same plan now. Just let me-"

175

"YOU had operational control?" She looked like he'd just spit on her grandma's grave or something. "So you didn't JUST sell us out??? YOU sent the team to murder my husband as well???"

Before I the last word came out of her mouth, I realized that Sivan was pointing her gun directly at his head. I spoke up, "Sivan, no!!"

Mrs. Katzav quickly glanced at her daughter. "Sivan, lower your weapon."

"He . . . killed . . . aba," she hissed through gritted teeth. Tears were welling up in her eyes. I think she was afraid she'd break down and openly cry in front of us if she opened her mouth at all.

"Sivan, your aba would not want you to kill him. Lower your weapon!!!"

"My aba would not want me and Amir growing up without him. This . . . man . . . took aba away."

"Sivan, put the damned gun down-"

"No!!!" Her hand was shaking. She really wanted to pull the trigger. Something inside her was preventing it . . . something that was hanging by a thread.

"He's an unarmed prisoner. If you kill him it's cold blood. If you kill him, it's murder."

"Like his team did to aba. It's right. It's JUSTICE. He should die. I watched aba's body fall to the ground. I watched . . . " she seemed to trail off.

Sivan's mom looked horrified to hear these words from her daughter. I had to pipe up . . . in my calmest voice possible, "Sivan, don't do this to yourself. It's not worth the nightmares. It's not worth what it does to you. It hurts like you wouldn't believe-"

"Shut up, Cohen!!! It's not your father he killed."

"Sivan, I'm not trying to save HIM. You have no idea what this will do to YOU."

"Shut!!! Up!!! Cohen!!!" She was whispering at a complete hiss—her teeth nearly chattering because she was shaking so badly.

Zippy had limped around to Sivan's other side. We now completely flanked her. Zippy spoke at a near whisper, "Sivan. You were there with me five years ago when I had the first nightmare, and the fiftieth, and the hundredth. Don't do this. You have no idea what's on the other side of that trigger pull."

The first tear streaked down Sivan's cheek. "I have to do this."

Sivan's mom said something in Hebrew. Dr. Shadad interrupted, "Ple- Please Sivan. Please don't do this. Nobody was ever supposed to die. They weren't supposed to kill your father. He wasn't supposed to be home."

He really needed to shut up. I never understood what it was about this shrink. He thought he could make me kill Zippy. Now he thinks he can keep Sivan from killing him. You can't talk your way through EVERYTHING, you know.

"It was just supposed to be a quick grab. Get in. Get you. Get out and ransom you. Your father just got in the way."

Holy hell, I can't believe he just said-

BANG!!! His head exploded from the side, splattering blood across the wall.

CHAPTER TWENTY-FOUR – BLOODBATH

Shadad's body slumped out of the chair and flopped onto the ground. Sivan dropped her gun to the floor. It took a second for me to realize she hadn't fired—her mom had!!! Mrs. Katzav turned to us and said, "One shot to the temple—just like the killing shot that took Shlomo from me."

His body spasmed on the floor for a few seconds, then it stopped. Mrs. Katzav walked over and emptied her clip into his dead body. "Just like they did to Shlomo."

Sivan fell to her knees with absolute horror on her face. I don't think she'd ever seen her mom kill someone. Zippy just stood there and watched.

Mrs. Katzav was nonchalant about it. You'd think she just stepped on a bug or something, instead of killing a man. "He was stalling. We've gotta get back to this mission before his boss tries to leave the country. Cohen, Dagan, go get the others and meet me in five minutes in the lobby downstairs. Sivan . . . Sivan???"

She just sat there, staring at the body.

179

"Kids, go get the others."

I knelt down and put my arm around Sivan. "I can't leave her behind-"

"Do as I say!! Get the others and meet with me. She's my daughter. She will be okay. Nothing will hurt her while I'm here. Now GO!!!"

I got up to walk out, but Sivan grabbed my arm and wouldn't let go. Her eyes still didn't leave Dr. Shadad's body.

"Fine. Will do it myself. Dagan, you're with me." Zippy and Mrs. Katzav headed to the door. As they walked out, Mrs. Katzav yelled, "You two be downstairs in five minutes." And they both left.

Sivan just put her arms around me. She never said a word. After a few minutes she finally stood up and took me by the hand. We walked out like a couple.

By the time we reached the others, she'd regained her composure. We were ready to go rescue a small child, stop another international terrorist, and hopefully put an end to this NSA nonsense before summer. Dammit, I wanted a vacation.

Sunday, March 11, 1991, 2:45 p.m.

The NSA traced Shadad's telephone calls to yet another hotel. This one was in Dallas. They immediately put adult agents on the hotel, watching it. M-Gang did away with our typical three-week plan and practice routine. We'd just done this mission once. We should be able to run the same drill again—just in a different town.

Zippy decided on a change of plans before we got to the hotel, though. She wanted Sheri and Danny to take up sniper positions. She wanted Aaron and Rachel to ensure that escape routes were open. And she wanted the rest of us on the primary mission, along with Mr. Jacobs who was going to be our "chaperone" up until the shooting starts.

But she wanted Amir to hold on to her backpack and to stay out of the way if any real fighting or shooting started. She didn't explain why.

Aaron protested, insisting that he be part of the primary team. This really aggravated Zippy and resulted in him limping for the entire afternoon.

We got to the hotel and saw that there were three guards outside the front door. They were wearing suits with earpieces and sunglasses. You couldn't have gotten any more obvious.

Mr. Jacobs got out of the van first, then the four M-Gang kids followed. We walked over to the guards and got their attention. The first guard ignored us completely. Mr. Jacobs addressed the second guard, "Excuse me. I'm trying to take these kids to the Wet and Wild Water Park. Can you tell me how to get there?" That sounded so good to me. Why couldn't the four of us just have an adult drop us off at Wet and Wild for the day? Why did we have to go around getting into fights for other people? Why did we have to kill for other people?

"Get lost!!!" This guard was NOT in the mood.

"Now, there's no need to be rude, sir. I'm just trying to"

"I SAID GET LOST!!" The second guard squared up on him like he was about to start a fight.

Zippy pleaded with the first guard, "Mister, please. Can't you help us find-" She slashed her hidden knife across his throat then kicked him in the groin as hard as she could. His hands had instinctively gone to his neck and he doubled over from the kick. Blood sprayed everywhere from his throat.

Sivan nailed the second guard with the stun gun. He went down immediately. She kept it attached to him, and set it to auto. It would zap him nonstop for thirty minutes unless she came back to turn it off.

The third guard had pulled a gun, I charged at him to buy Zippy a few seconds. He turned and aimed it at me.

He never saw Zippy race up behind him. With one hand, she grabbed him by the hair. With her other hand, she stabbed her knife right into the side of his throat—right through the jugular. Then she punched her hand forward, shooting the knife through the front of his throat, severing his windpipe from behind, and nearly decapitating him. Hot blood splattered across all of our faces.

The coms crackled, Rachael shouted "Zippy, there's a fourth guard 20 feet to your left!!! He's spotted you."

Before any of us could react, Mr. Jacobs ran at him, screaming like a banshee at the top of his lungs. SLAM!!!! Jacobs crashed into the guard, launching him several feet backwards.

Zippy and Sivan sprinted after them. Mr. Jacobs jumped on top of the guy, and started punching him in the face. He didn't see the man pull a tactical knife out of his right pocket.

Sivan got to them just in time and stepped on the guard's wrist. Zippy pushed Jacobs out of the way and-

Splat!!!

Zippy threw herself to the ground, making sure her knee landed right in the middle of the guard's face. Then she slashed downward three times, sufficiently opening up his throat. She stayed there for a few seconds with her knee on his face and a pool of blood forming on the ground around them.

She turned around and grabbed Jacobs by the lapel. "LOOK. LOOK down next to you." He looked down to see Sivan's foot, in her little brown tasseled penny-loafers, standing on the guard's knife-wielding hand. "You nearly got yourself KILLED!! You don't do violence. We do violence. You just stand there and look scary. You understand???"

Mr. Jacobs was in complete shock. He had no idea how closely he'd cheated death. "I- I just wanted to pull my weight."

Sivan took a few steps back. The guard was dead, and the pool of blood was getting dangerously close to her feet.

Zippy continued. "Mr. Jacobs, it is a terrible burden to kill someone. People say it darkens your heart. People say it makes you dirty inside. But they're wrong. It doesn't DARKEN your heart. It tears it. Killing someone cuts your heart and leaves a scar. I have killed many men. Each one has torn that scar open and hurt me just a little more. That scar will never go away. Mark knows what I mean."

She looked up at me. I nodded in agreement.

"I don't want anyone taking a life on this mission unless they have to. No scars!!! If killing is to be done, I will do it or Mark will. We have both killed. It will hurt us less. Nobody else gets their hearts scarred tonight. You understand?"

He nodded. Zippy and I both turned and headed back for the entrance. Amir had been standing there, keeping watch the entire time. Sivan just stood there for a minute, staring at the guard's dead body. She muttered the words "no scars" under her breath, then offered Mr. Jacobs a hand, helping him to his feet.

We went into the hotel and walked right past that front desk. Nobody questions four kids in the custody of one big adult chaperone. We got to the elevator and Zippy turned to Mr. Jacobs. "This is as far as you go with us. There is true darkness where we're going. Go to our room that NSA booked for us, and wait for us to return with the child."

He didn't argue. We all got on the elevator, and dropped Mr. Jacobs off on the third floor. Then it was just the four of us. Zippy told Amir to stay by the elevator. He protested, but she said something about a stray bullet making a mess of him. I had no idea what she was talking about.

We got to the 12th floor. Zippy, Sivan and I went down the hallway which was curiously free of any guards. I guess

Benson like to keep his guards outside the building for some reason. We made our way to the Presidential Suite. Why did these bad guys always manage to get such awesome rooms?

We formed up outside the doorway just like we had in Fort Worth, only now there was just the three of us. Zippy carefully started to open the door when suddenly she stopped and said, "Damn!!!" She looked back at Sivan and whispered, "It's latched."

Sivan knew exactly what to do. She handed me two flash-grenades from her backpack, then whispered "stand aside." She stepped back and launched her entire body forward in one move, kicking the door as hard as she could. The door frame around the latch cracked completely off the wall, and the door flew wide open. I threw the first flash grenade and we all covered our ears and shut our eyes.

BANG!!!

The windows blew out in the living room and the television screen shattered. Zippy and I rushed in. There were two guards. They were just standing there looking at the floor, completely stunned.

BANG, BANG, BANG, BANG!!!

We took out one guard each, putting two rounds in each chest and one into each head. As soon as the last guard fell, I ran towards the bedroom door and threw a flash grenade inside. We covered our ears and looked away.

BANG!

Zippy ran into the bedroom first with her gun drawn. I followed. What greeted us was the most horrible thing I'd seen in my entire life!!! I can't even really describe what I saw him doing to that little girl. And I'm not going to even try. But sufficed to say, I couldn't help myself. I was so disgusted. I couldn't say anything. I couldn't even throw-up. I just pointed my gun center-mass on him, took a breath, and-

"NO!!!" Zippy screamed.

BANG!!!

She knocked my hand upward just in time. The safety-slug bullet I'd loaded into my gun shattered on the ceiling. "He's MINE!!!" She immediately turned and pointed her gun at him, "Do not move, Mr. Benson!!! I am Tsipporah Dagan from Mossad, and I am more than eager to kill you. How painful a death you suffer will depend on how well you cooperate." He was still suffering the effects of the flash-grenade, and looked wholly confused. Zippy turned back at me with a disturbing seriousness, "We do not to kill him yet!!! Sivan, get in here!!!"

The little girl was crying when Sivan came running through the door.

"Sivan, the kid." Zippy really didn't need to say anything else.

Sivan ran over to the little girl and picked her up. In a voice more high-pitched and baby-friendly than I'd ever heard come out of Sivan, she started soothing the child, "Hi Eliana. I'm Sivan. You're safe now." She yanked the sheet of the other bed in the room and started wrapping the child up in it.

Sivan just couldn't stand to take the child out naked. "We're going to go see your mommy and daddy. Okay?" The child had stopped crying. "Do you want to go see mommy? Here . . ." she pulled out a piece of candy from her pocket and put it in the little girl's mouth.

Once Sivan had the youngster completely bundled up, she swooped her up and ran out of the room holding the kid tightly to her chest. She blurted into the coms, "Amir, cover them. I've got the Hadawi girl. I'm taking her to the safe room."

Zippy tapped her coms, "Amir, belay that. Bring me my backpack." Amir showed up a few seconds later with Zippy's backpack and handed it to her. "Todah. Now, get yourself back to the safe room. Try to close what's left of the door behind you as you leave." He obeyed without question.

Now it was time for us to turn our attention to Benson. He'd started to shake off the effects of the flash-grenade.

Zippy opened up her backpack and pulled out two sets of handcuffs. She threw them at Benson and pointed her gun at his privates. "Handcuff yourself to the bedpost."

He cuffed his right hand to a bedpost, but had trouble with his left. His hands were shaking—residual effects from the grenade. He looked back at Zippy and said "I can't cuff this hand because the other hand is already cuffed."

She smiled, sympathetically.

BANG!!! BANG!!! She shot each of his ankles. He screamed like a lady. The smile never left Zippy's face.

"Now that we know you're not going anywhere. Please slap the other cuff to the bedpost. Or do I need to make other parts of you explode?" He was shaking, screaming, and calling her every four-letter word ever uttered, but he got the other cuff slapped on. Zippy then had me tie what was left of his ankles down to the bed.

Zippy pulled two jugs of hydrochloric acid out of her backpack. No wonder she wanted Amir away from the firefight. Imagine if one of those had gotten hit by a stray bullet!!! She also pulled out a stun-gun, two mace cans, a garlic-mincer, and her little pouch full of syringes. Maybe I was finally going to find out what was in them.

"Now Mr. Benson, let's talk."

CHAPTER TWENTY-FIVE – AM I A MONSTER?

He was panting, hysterically. I imagine having two joints blasted out with a 9mm gun will do that to you.

"I'd like to talk about two things. First, I'd like to discuss your connections with Savak. Then I'd like to share with you my opinion of men who hurt little girls." She snapped the garlic-mincer and put it on the table, before slowly pulling one of the syringes out of the pouch.

Looking over at Benson like she expected him to be talking already, she asked "Nothing, Mr. Benson?" Her voice sounded disturbingly playful, "If you knew what I was about to inject you with, you might think about speaking up."

"You can go to hell!!! I'm not begging some damned kike kid for my life. Especially one who pretends to be from the likes of Mossad."

She suddenly turned serious, "I am Mossad, Mr. Benson. You're not the first to fatally misunderstand that. Two Savak grab teams have already failed-"

"The hell you are!!!" he barked. Didn't his mother tell

187

him not to interrupt the professional assassin who's about to torture him to death? This guy was either crazy or stupid!!!

Zippy's voice lowered to a near whisper, "When I torture you to death, will it matter whether you believe me? Perhaps you've heard of me. In Israel, they called me the 'angel of death.' I have killed a dozen men in my life." She leaned in towards him, "You will be the first one I've actually enjoyed killing. Now, I have questions. And you WILL answer them." She sounded like Sivan's mom.

I guess he thought we were bluffing. He shook his head with disbelief, "I'm not talking, kike. I don't care what you threaten me-"

Zippy injected the syringe into his thigh. The scream he let out was horrific. He started writhing in the bed.

"Like I said, I have strong feelings about men who hurt little girls." She went back to the pouch, "I'm going to make this painful, Mr. Benson. You are going to be in severe agony for the remainder of our conversation. How severe depends on you, and how well you answer my questions."

She carefully removed the second syringe from her pouch. She looked almost like a nurse, slowly giving the patient his medicine. Her facial expression never changed. She kept the same gentle smile on throughout the entire process. That was scary. "The diamondback rattlesnake, Mr. Benson. It's the most aggressive pit-viper in the North American continent. Its venom is chemically no different from the venom of a red-wasp. The only difference between a wasp and a serpent is the serpent injects a thousand times as much as a wasp ever could."

She walked over to his other side. "It's cytotoxic, meaning it destroys your cells on contact. Now the red-wasp's sting is extremely painful, but the snake's venom is incapacitating. And each of these syringes contains five times the venom of a single snake-bite." She injected his other thigh. His screams could have woken the dead.

"Now, I'll let that sink in for a minute. As I said, I have questions. You would be wise to answer them." She just stood there watching for a few minutes, watching him writhe like a fish out of water, squirming as it suffocates. Then she removed another syringe from the pouch. "I would very much like to know who your contact in the middle-east is."

She walked over to him with it and waited for his screams to die down a bit. He was starting to shiver. I think the snake-toxin was starting to affect him all over. "Would you be so kind as to give me a name?"

"Sa- Salimah!!! Her name is Salimah"

Zippy shook her head and clicked her tongue a few times. Then she started injecting his right underarm. "Nice try, Mr. Benson. But I killed Adara Salimah last summer." His increasingly hoarse screams were horrifying. Zippy stood there for a minute, examining her work, then she returned to the pouch to pull out another syringe.

Benson looked like he was going to pass out. He was desperately trying to speak in between gasps, panting madly, "It- It's not- It's not Adara. It's her- her sister, Sahara!!!"

Zippy and I looked at each other, stunned. Zippy put on a poker face—not that she needed to, given how Benson was falling apart—and continued to question him, "So Adara Salimah has a sister. And how did you get involved with her?"

"Her team was trying to figure out how to remotely take over American 'Patriot' missiles. She found Shadad through Shamil Hassan's network of contacts. Shadad knew that Hadawi was a key engineer on the missile's guidance system. They wanted to take this engineer's kid and hold her ransom so that they could make him turn over some technical info. They found me because I've got a trafficking network for . . ."

"Yes?"

He hesitated. We knew what his organization did. There was no sense in trying to hide it. But that didn't stop him from trying to sugar-coat it, "I connect lonely men in other countries with . . ."

"Unwilling girls?"

"Please . . . PLEASE," he was openly sobbing, "they kidnapped the little girl. It wasn't me. They wanted me to hold onto her until Salimah could arrange funds for transport. They used me. They knew what I was. They knew what I'd do. They . . . please."

"Where can I find Salimah?"

He spilled his guts . . . figuratively. We literally spilled them later, but that wasn't for a little while. He detailed every facet of his human trafficking network and Sahara Salimah's terrorist funding network. The whole time he talked, Zippy stood over him, holding a syringe filled with venom. When he was finished, she motioned like she was about to inject his other underarm.

"PLEASE . . . I told you everything!!!" His voice was so hoarse that my throat hurt just listening. He was shaking, and not from fear. The venom was killing him. He was starting to show signs of shock. By my count, Zippy had injected him with the equivalent of at least 15 rattlesnake bites at this point. Who survives that?

Zippy's voice took on the air of a teacher who was scolding a naughty student. "Yes, so now we move on to the next topic: my feelings regarding men who hurt little girls." She injected his left underarm. He screamed till his voice went out. At this point, he was flat out convulsing and going in and out of consciousness.

Zippy looked over at me. She seemed sad. "Am I a monster?"

That question surprised me. Why would she ask something like that? I shook my head and responded with a definite, "No way. Why would you ever think-"

"Mark, I just tortured a man. The information he gave

was not urgent. We could have let the adults interrogate him and get it all. But I tortured him."

"Zippy, you saw what he was doing."

"Yeah, but then look at what I did. In a few minutes, his body will give out, and I will have tortured a man to death. He was a monster, no doubt. I'm just afraid . . . I'm afraid that I'm becoming every bit as much of a monster as these men I've killed."

"Well, he's not dead yet. You can still call an ambulance and try to save him."

She sighed. "Yeah, and maybe that's the worst part. I just don't want to save him. Maybe I am becoming a monster. I've killed men less bad than him." She looked over at his shivering body, "I just don't feel like lifting a finger to save him."

"Neither do I. Maybe I'm becoming a monster too."

"Yeah," a tear streaked down her cheek, "It's just . . . someone like that just shouldn't be alive—not after what I saw him doing to that little girl. I just don't . . . I don't want to become something that's just as bad."

"If so, then we're both bad. You know what we saw wasn't his debut at hurting little girls like that." I reminded her, "and if we save him, it won't be his finale either. Like I told Mr. Jacobs, we kill bad people to keep them from hurting innocent people."

"Yeah. I told him the same thing." She got up and headed for the living room. I noticed she was limping ever so slightly.

"Are you alright? You're limping."

She smiled, "Yeah, Sivan knows how to take someone out alright." She pointed down to the huge black spot on her thigh. "But I don't get to complain after what I did to you.

"Zippy, I'm going to be alright."

"Yeah. I still feel terrible, though. Like I said, I don't want to become a monster." Then she smiled again, "But it looks like Katzav has a few moves I didn't know about."

I chuckled, "Yep. She and her mom developed some special moves for the 'Ladies Self Defense' thing. That one she got you with is called 'the boyfriend' shot."

"The boyfriend???" Zippy looked insulted.

"Yeah, it's for girls who want to win the fight, but don't want to rack the guy. You lock up for a knee, then throw it into the thigh. It incapacitates him. And it stands as a warning shot. You know, 'you see how bad this hurt—the next one goes into your balls' and such."

"Hmmm." Zippy thought for a second, "I never saw that coming. She's been holding out on me. I'm going to have to see what else she's developed. We used to share all our moves with each other." We walked into the living room, and Zippy buzzed her coms, "Sivan, come in. Come in Katzav." Nothing. "Katzav, are you there?" Still nothing.

A voice came from the doorway, "She turned it off!!!" We both spun around, aiming our guns. It was Amir. We both lowered our weapons and breathed a sigh.

Zippy was annoyed, "Don't sneak up on us like that!!! I told you to go back to our room!!! And what the hell do you mean 'she turned them off??' We NEVER disable coms during a mission like that!!"

Amir looked over at Benson then looked back at Zippy. "The ambulance arrived, but the kid wouldn't let go of Sivan. She just clung to Sivan's arm like her life depended on it. She was screaming and begging Sivan not to leave her, so Sivan got into the ambulance with the kid and went to the hospital with her." He looked over at Benson.

Zippy insisted, "Amir, you need to get out of here. I don't want you to-"

"Be a part of what you're doing to him? Zippy, I've killed men too. Last year, I shot two of Adara's guards in the elevator shaft. They were trying to kill Sarah." He looked over at me, "You were busy getting beaten up by

Adara. And I killed those men." He looked back at Zippy, "You don't have to protect me from killing. You should have let me get more involved tonight.

Zippy chuckled, "Amir, there were two gallons of hydrochloric acid in your backpack. One stray bullet to that backpack and your entire body would have been melted. I wasn't protecting you from having to kill someone. I was simply protecting you."

Amir seemed to shrink a bit. Zippy continued, "And Benson is going to die any minute now. I've poisoned him. I don't want it on your conscience. So you should go now."

"What did you poison him with?"

Zippy refused to answer, so I did it for her, "Rattlesnake venom—about 20 bites worth."

Amir chuckled, "A man is mortally wounded. He cannot be saved. There's nothing I can do for him. Even if I were a doctor, he's going to die. So how would he be on my conscience?"

Zippy nodded.

The coms crackled back, "Kids, this is Sanders. The Hadawi kid's parents have been contacted. Give me an update on Benson."

Zippy waited a minute, "This is Dagan. He's alive but injured. It's mortal. Don't bother with an ambulance. He'll be dead in minutes and there's nothing any of us can do to stop that. I've got a cleaning kit here. I'll let you know when we're done."

After Benson stopped wheezing and convulsing, Zippy picked up the jugs of acid, then looked over at me and Amir, "Now comes the hard part."

I was so glad she stopped me from shooting him. I'd like to think that the moment he got to hell, it was a relief.

CHAPTER TWENTY-SIX – THE
GUARDIAN ANGEL

Friday, May 31, 1991

So there I was, sitting in front of yet another therapist. She was in her early-30s. Her hair was bright red. She wore thick, round glasses, and was insanely beautiful. I was going to have a hard time talking to her about stuff. I didn't want to cry in front of someone so hot.

Two weeks ago, I firmly refused to see another damned therapist, and told Sanders just what he could do with himself before even trying to make me sit in this chair.

Then I got a phone call from Israel. It was Sarah Rabin, the Shabak agent who oversaw all of our missions last year. She told me that a very dear friend of hers from the Shabak profiling unit was heading for the US to help the M-Gang kids work through some . . . stuff. This Shabak profiler was named Dr. April Levitt. Sarah promised me that I could trust this person, and asked me to please give her a chance. Sarah is one of the few people in this world I truly trust . . . even though she failed to tell me how attractive her friend was. Should have known, though. I've yet to meet an Israeli female who hasn't made my heart ache.

So there I was, yet again, in front of a therapist.

"Before we start, do you have any questions for me?" She had a gentle style. For just a moment, it reminded me of Shadad and I almost put my guard up. I actually had a million questions for her, but there was one that was burning through, and I was afraid to ask it. But what the hell, here goes . . .

"Dr. Levitt,"

"Mark, we're going to be friends. Call me April." She flashed a completely disarming smile.

"Okay . . . April . . . Why is it every time somebody makes up sex-stuff about me, everyone believes it?"

She sat back, "You certainly get to the point, don't you?"

"Well, it keeps happening. I keep getting hurt, and I just wanted to know if it was something about me. You know? Are my parents right? Should I be doing something or acting some way to make people not think things like that?"

"No. If you take nothing else from all of our time together, you must learn that none of this was your fault. Mark, I've read all the incident reports. I've seen the spy-cam videos Shadad made of all his sessions with you and the other kids. NONE of this was your fault."

"But this wasn't the first time someone made up sex-stuff about me."

"I know. I read Tsipporah's report on you from last year—the one where she recommended your recruitment."

I never really thought about Zippy writing a "report" on me. That felt kinda weird.

"But to answer your question, it's not something that's unique to you. There's something innately dark about human nature. When someone is accused of something, we typically want to believe it."

She paused for a second, like she was trying to carefully

pick out the right words, "This is especially true when you accuse someone of sexual wrongdoing. For some reason people want to believe accusations when they involve rape, molestation, or other bad acts involving sex. People kneejerk to believe it. Even if someone can prove that they're innocent. Even if there's a big trial and the police get involved and the accused is proven innocent, people still hold a secret belief, deep down inside, that this guy or girl really did what they were accused of."

She leaned forward, "Back in Israel, I have counseled multiple men who have been wrongfully accused of horrible acts involving sex. Their lives were turned upside down. They were treated terribly. And every one of them was innocent. Nothing I can tell you will take away the pain of what you've experienced. Nothing I can tell you will make it hurt less when you think about it—especially the betrayal by those who listened and believed the allegations."

She opened her file folder, "M-Gang incident reports show that last year, some kids were making prank calls to some girl's house and pretending to be you."

I nodded.

"At one point, the police got involved."

I nodded again.

"They proved that it was some other kid. But I'd be willing to bet you never got an apology, did you?"

I shook my head.

"Tsipporah Dagan put the girl's father in the emergency room. Right?"

I smiled, "I don't think she took it quite that far."

"But you recall, she accused him of fondling her. That was also a false allegation of sexual wrongdoing."

That thought made me uncomfortable. I didn't like to think of Zippy doing things like that.

"It's a weapon—these allegations. Female agents sometimes make them, but only as situations require. When everyday people make up such intentional lies, for no reason other than to hurt someone, it's just as much of a wrong as hitting someone, shooting someone, stabbing them, vandalizing their property . . . it should be a crime, and in fact is a crime in many places."

She took off her glasses, "And that brings us to you. You've been the victim of a terrible wrong—three times by my count. Once at your school when those kids made up those stories about you. Once when those kids made those prank calls. And once from Shadad's doing. The real question is how deeply you were hurt. How much damage has been done to you?"

She leaned even further forward, "Can you trust your friends again?"

"I don't know. Zippy didn't mean to . . . but she did believe stuff . . . I don't know. It's hard. It's confusing."

She smiled, "And that's what you and I will explore over the next few weeks. You strike me as a very trusting young man. And that's a good thing. Tsipporah, Sheri, Danny, Rachael . . . they're lucky. You'll probably be able to trust them again. Do you want to?"

I nodded again. "I don't want to NOT trust my friends. I just don't want to . . . I don't want to get hurt again. I don't want this whole thing to have been for nothing. I don't want to get hurt, then let myself get hurt again."

"Good," she responded, "that's a good place to start. You'll get plenty of opportunity. I've been informed that you and the other M-Gang kids will be spending the entire summer together on the beaches of Florida. Tel Aviv thinks you need a break, and some fun, so they've booked a small hotel for you kids, Mrs. Katzav, and the Dagans."

I perked up. This sounded good!!! "You mean, we get the entire summer just to ourselves."

"After what you've all just been through, even the American government agreed to chip in."

And so it began. April and I started working on putting me back together again.

Sunday, June 2, 1991, 9:15 a.m.

Zippy, Sivan, and I arrived at Plano General Hospital. I really wanted to walk away from this mission, but some pencil-pusher somewhere agreed to let Eliana's parents meet with these youngsters who worked so hard to rescue their daughter.

True to his word, Aaron quit the M-Gang the day after we killed Benson. He wanted no more of it, and who could blame him. We all felt like quitting. That's probably why they brought April in. The rest of the M-Gang kids had spent the last two months going out of their way to be extra-nice to me. It was like a daily celebration of all things Mark. I can't say that I minded. We also attended group-therapy sessions with April, which helped fix a lot of things.

I finally got fed-up with Collins, and being told I was going to hell for . . . pick one: reading a Bible other than the "King James Translation;" listening to rock music; watching horror movies; having a Jewish last name; spending all my time with Jewish kids; or just being me. My parents are going to enroll me in Thorne high school this summer. Sivan's mom is going to enroll her and Amir there as well. No more private school for the three of us.

Not that school was on any of our minds. We were all looking forward to our Florida trip, which was leaving tomorrow. All we had to do was tie-off this one loose end. We had to meet with Eliana's parents.

I hated being inside this hospital—I couldn't help but remember all the times little Elise nearly died here. Fortunately, nobody notices a bunch of 13-year olds walking in. We walked right passed the nurses station, onto the secure wing where the little girl was staying. We immediately spotted the adult crew.

The NSA guys on hand had just finished reading the parents in when we arrived. This annoyed the hell out of me. Why don't we just read in the whole damned world?!?! Tell everyone about M-Gang!!! Sheesh.

Mr. Jacobs was there. He was getting a little too comfortable with his new position. He ushered us into a private lobby-like room where the parents were wrapping up their discussions with the NSA. "Mr. and Mrs. Hadawi, these are Agents Dagan, Katzav, and Cohen."

It was like a middle-east peace conference. Here were three Jews, two of which were Israeli, talking to two Palestinians; while all being moderated by an American Baptist who really had no business being there. And like so many other things I've done, nobody would ever know.

Mrs. Hadawi immediately ran over and hugged each one of us. She was crying her eyes out and thanking us profusely. She knew we'd worked on finding her daughter, but she had no idea we were the breach team. I can't imagine how she'd respond if she found out that little nugget.

Mr. Hadawi was completely silent. After Sivan, Zippy, and Mrs. Hadawi started a conversation on Eliana's recovery, he pulled me aside for a little "man talk."

"These guys," he said, pointing towards the NSA officers who were standing outside the door, "they tell me that I can't confront the man who . . . the man who RUINED my daughter." He was gritting his teeth and trying desperately to keep his voice at a whisper. It kinda reminded me of my little confrontation with Mr. Peters at the orchestra competition a lifetime ago. "Can you tell me anything about him? I want to face him. I want to KILL this man. I want his blood." He was getting extremely worked up and I was gesturing for him to calm down before he got too loud. But he kept going " . . . and these damned . . . BUSINESS SUITS say I can't even attend his trial."

"Well, sir, there's not going to be a trial."

He grabbed my lapel, I had to motion quickly to keep

Zippy and Sivan from running over. I could handle this.

"What do you mean, they're letting him-"

"Nothing. They're not letting him do anything." Now I was getting intense. I made a judgment call on the spot – what the hell, he's already read-in. "Do you know exactly what it is the three of us did to get your daughter back?"

He looked at me, quite puzzled. I put on my best bored face, just like I'd been taught, "We weren't just intelligence. We didn't just go freeze our tails off in the downtown area last February while looking for her. We had direct contact with the-"

"You've SEEN this man?!?!? When???"

"Recently, look that's not the important part. What you need to know is-"

"So he's nearby. Please . . . she's my daughter. I have to . . . where is he?"

Time for another judgment call, "He's in a lot of places. Zippy and I left pieces of him all over Plano, Richardson, Addison, Carrollton, Los Colinas-"

The look of shock on his face was worth every single moment of this wretched mission.

"Do not play with me!! I am serious-" His voice had taken on a whole new character.

I looked straight into his eyes, feigning as much boredom as humanly possible, "So am I. Do you have any idea who we are?"

He shook his head no.

"We're the Mossad Youth. We don't take prisoners. We aren't just intelligence. We're operational counter-terror. We were . . . Agent Dagan and I 'interrogated' him after we rescued Eliana."

"And?"

"And he won't be hurting any more little girls. He won't be hurting anyone for that matter."

He looked like someone had just whacked him with a baseball bat.

"Do you see Agent Dagan over there?" I felt weird calling her that. "She's forgotten more about causing horrific pain, suffering, and shocking damage to the human body than the scariest people in the world ever knew." I'm not sure that was much of an exaggeration. "She and I took our time with him. I won't tell you what all we did, but he lost his voice from the screaming long before he died."

Mr. Hadawi smiled at that, so I figured I'd go on. "Zippy can cause so much pain in a single moment that a man throws up. She took her time with this guy. I've never seen her achieve such levels of cruelty."

Okay, now there was absolute satisfaction on his face.

"So believe me, he suffered a thousand times more than what he did to little Ellie." Now, time for the gold, "We also killed the man who gave his team your address, and we've killed everyone involved. So you see, there's nothing left for you to do but love your daughter. Help her heal. Help her forget."

It took him a few moments, but he finally nodded as though he understood. So we rejoined the others.

Sivan . . . I mean . . . Agent Katzav was doing her best to keep Mrs. Hadawi calm, but it wasn't working.

"The doctors say she was drugged and . . . and he touched her!!! She's only six!!! What kind of monster does something like that?!?!?"

We just let her continue. No need to try to calm her down. Just let her get it all out.

"They still don't know what all drugs he gave her," she said with a sigh of resignation. "She's still having hallucinations. I guess I should be thankful for that. She doesn't remember much of what 'the bad man' did to her. But she remembers some sketchy details of her rescue . . ."

She started sobbing, "My little Ellie . . . I don't know what's real and what she's imagining . . . she said the door blew up, and there were loud bangs, and shouting, and these scary people ran in and-" her voice cracked "and then she said that an angel swooped in and saved her."

She completely broke down. "I know it sounds crazy but . . ."

Nah, I kinda like the sound of that.

". . . but she's so sincere. She doesn't cry. She just sits there like she's explaining some new word she's learned. It's so . . . precious."

Mr. Hadawi put his arm around his wife, who had one last bit to tell us, "She says the angel carried her off and made everything okay. She says she's not afraid of anything anymore. Any time she wakes up scared, she just remembers that an angel is there to save her. She calls the angel 'Sivan.' Do you have any idea why she calls her that?" Zippy and I put on our best poker faces and started with a cover story. No need for these two to ever know anything about what we walked in on. Sivan turned and walked away. I don't think she could stand the notion of either me or Zippy ever seeing her cry.

EPILOGUE – THE SVELTE ASSASSIN

Sunday, August 18, 1991

Sivan was sitting on the arm of the couch in the M-Gang lounge. She was wearing a glittery spandex top, with shiny tan tights that made her legs look even longer (as if that were possible) and these dance shoes which looked more like vinyl sox than anything you'd ever call a shoe. She was swinging her legs back and forth, pointing her toes forward and examining her feet as though she was trying to figure out some secret they might be holding. Her hair was pulled tight into a pony tail, and she had so much makeup on that it almost looked clownish, with outrageously bright red lipstick. It took me a few seconds to even recognize her . . . and another few seconds to realize just how impossibly gorgeous she was to me at this very moment. My heart literally ached for her. Was this what it felt like when a guy realizes he really likes a girl?

At the same time, she also looked a bit sad, or maybe she was just tired. Either way, she seemed to brighten up a bit when I walked in.

"Hi Mark." Wow, even her voice sounded exhausted.

"What's up, Sivan?" The message she'd left on my parents' answering machine sounded urgent, but by now I'd already forgotten that, given the spectacle in front of me. She immediately realized just how much I'd noticed her new look.

"I registered at Thorne High School this morning. The Sveltes, are having tryouts this afternoon. I talked to Angela. She spoke with the coach and got me a spot in the tryouts. I'm going for it."

After my brain reassembled itself from the shock, I finally managed to string together a sentence, "Uh . . . weren't you afraid of everyone else finding out about your secret dance habit?" Okay, that sounded stupid, but it's all I could manage to spit out.

"Well – not anymore. Besides, fear is a lousy excuse for not doing things you enjoy."

She looked back down, and continued to study her feet "And at least there I'm not going to hurt people. At least there I'm . . ."

I tried to finish the sentence for her "-going to be hanging out with a bunch of glorified cheerleaders, who stab you in the back, gossip, and are generally mean to you and everyone around you?"

She smirked a bit, "Well . . . aside from the fact that you just described what M-Gang was like last year, I think I can handle it. After all, if I can handle international terrorist organizations-"

"Yeah. You're a trained assassin. Are you sure joining a dance team is going to be good for the health and safety of those poor girls?"

She laughed, "I am indeed trained—a fact which will become readily apparent to any sports jock who thinks this outfit makes me an easy mark. But an assassin? No. I'm no assassin. Tsipporah is an assassin, and she's good at it. You're an assassin, and you're good at it. It's just something that I don't have in me . . . and I've tried and tried to grasp it. It's just not something I'm cut out for. And now I'm not so sure it's something I even want."

"Sivan, we've spent the last month together in Florida. You never said anything about not being sure about what it is we do. You never said-" I didn't know how to finish the sentence. I didn't like where this conversation was going.

After a lengthy pause, she finally piped back up, "You need to know the reason why I hated you when we first met. Some of the M-Gangers made you think it's because you're Ashkenazi. Mark, it's not just because you're Ashkenazi. Rachael is Ashkenazi. Danny is Ashkenazi. I've always liked them. You were . . . It was something else."

A tear came rolling down, painting a black makeup streak on her cheek. "You know about Zippy killing the Savak team." Her voice cracked. "They murdered my Aba."

This was scary. I'd never seen Sivan outright cry—not even when she was holding that gun on Shadad. She actually looked vulnerable.

"And I watched it happen!!! They found my family first. I was running away and I turned around just in time to see them-" She couldn't finish the sentence—she was beginning to really sob now.

"They got to your family a week before they went after Zippy. I know, Sivan." I tried to be comforting, but I just didn't know what to say. I tried to hug her but she shoved me away.

"NO YOU DON'T!!!" She sat there staring for a few seconds, breathing more heavily than I'd ever seen, "You don't know . . . You don't know that our families were in Dallas because they were protecting YOU!! You were the 'kidnap target' five years ago that Shadad was talking about!!!"

What???

"Zippy said that Shamil Hassan tried to tell you before

you killed him last year. She lied to you and said she didn't know what he was talking about. Your parents—remember him saying something about your parents?"

Wow. I'd never told anyone but Shadad about that. And yeah, Zippy had denied knowing anything when I asked her. But Hassan did say something about them being involved and me not knowing.

"Your dad was working on some top secret project for the US government at his job. Terrorist chatter named you and your sister in a kidnap plot. Mossad . . . 'moved some assets' to assist the American government in its efforts to protect your family. That's why we were in Dallas. That's why Tsipporah's family was here. My aba died because he was protecting YOU!!!" I couldn't tell if it was rage, hatred, or sheer pain in her eyes.

"That's why I hated you!! I blamed you!! Who was this boy who was so damned precious that my aba had to die? Why did I have to lose my aba while you and your family went on without even knowing??"

She paused for a moment then looked back up at me, "I met Tsipporah the week after she killed the Iranian team. I was so jealous of her. My parents never trained me. My parents never taught me. They thought it was inappropriate for a child to learn about creating death. I was so jealous of her: she knew everything about how to fight . . . she saved her imeh, she saved her aba, she saved . . . she avenged my aba. She did what I never could. She killed those . . . she killed them."

"Sivan, that hurt her in way's you can't underst-"

"I know that!! I knew her back then. My family and I lived with the Dagans for several months. I was there when she'd wake up screaming every night. I was there when she'd talk about this little boy that she was going to protect. She was obsessed with you, Mark. It got really scary. She had this delusion that she was supposed to be like some sort of guardian angel." She huffed. "She never knew that the little boy she saw getting beaten up on that playground was the same little boy our parents were there to protect. Neither did I. Then we all went to your house that Saturday last year to recruit you. You seemed like such a scared little boy . . . I thought it would be cruel to introduce you to M-Gang, Krav fighting, and the things we were preparing for."

She paused again, "The next morning, my imeh and Tsipporah's parents sat us down and told us that this little boy Tsipporah wanted to recruit was the same little boy that they had been protecting all those years ago." She looked up at me. "I didn't really take that news very well. On one hand, I felt like Tsipporah was going to get you killed and I needed to protect you from that. But at the same time, I truly hated you . . . and I couldn't tell you because they forbad it. I had to watch Tsipporah play out her sick 'guardian angel' fantasy with the boy I'd spent four years HATING with every fiber of my being."

"And now there's a little girl out there who calls YOU the angel." I was trying to be helpful.

"Yeah. And now there are two Israeli girls who owe you more than you'll ever know."

That seemed oddly cryptic.

"You saved Tsipporah's life in the café that night. But you saved my . . . you saved my soul."

That phrase sounded downright unnatural coming from her.

"Mark . . ." She reached out and caressed my cheek. ". . . I joined this . . . this M-Gang insanity for one reason: to avenge my aba. Zippy killed the team that murdered him. But I wanted to hunt down and kill the man who sent them . . . and the man who sold them out. I never thought about how much it hurts your heart to take a human life. I never thought about the nightmares Tsipporah kept having, when she would wake up screaming at the top of her lungs. I never thought about the strange angry outbursts she'd have.

I always just thought that was part of who she was. But something happened on that day five years ago that truly broke her . . . it scarred her soul when she pulled that trigger. And I was so blinded by my range and hatred for the men who murdered my aba that I never thought about what it would do to me to get the revenge I wanted."

Hearing this kind of talk out of Sivan made me want to cry.

"Mark, you killed the man who sent the team that murdered my aba. My imeh killed the man who sold them out. You both took that scar for me. My reason for joining this mess is completed, and I've gotten away without that scar . . . and if I stay here I'm likely to collect that scar before it's over . . . and you will have suffered for nothing."

She turned away for a second, then looked directly into my eyes. The pain behind those upside-down eyelashes was horrific. "Mark, I quit the M-Gang this morning. I told my imeh and I told the Dagans already."

"Sivan, no! You can't just-"

"Mark, it's already done. I'm through with the violence. I don't need it anymore. My aba is avenged. The world is in good hands with you and Dagan . . . I'm just not cut-out to kill people. I don't have it in me . . . and too many people have suffered that experience . . . protecting me from it, for me to go on and force myself to kill someone. I can't do it, Mark. I just can't. I'm sorry."

She got up off the sofa's arm and started to walk out. "For what it's worth, I really like you Cohen. I hope my first boyfriend is a lot like you . . . hell, maybe you and I will be . . ."

She reached out and caressed my cheek again. I thought she was about to kiss me. She whispered, "I could do a lot worse. Maybe . . ." She stopped herself before saying anything she might later regret.

She smiled and started towards the door, "I'd make a much better girlfriend than Dagan, anyway. She'd break you balls for even trying to kiss her." She smiled. "I'd at least make out with you first . . . then I'd only break them if I found out you'd gone and told some damned shrink about it."

We both chuckled, which was hard because we both wanted to cry.

She stopped at the door. "I . . . you know."

"I know. I'll miss you." I was getting seriously choked up.

"Yeah . . . well, maybe I'll . . . I'll see you around, Cohen."

With that, Sivan walked out the door, leaving it half-opened. I just stood there, completely shattered. She'd been my best friend for the last year. She'd stood by me when even Zippy turned her back on me. Sivan had turned out to be the strongest, kindest, and most good-hearted person I'd ever known. And now she was gone.

For the first time since I joined, M-Gang was truly broken . . .

ABOUT THE AUTHOR

Robert Linus Koehl was born just outside of San Antonio, Texas, during the United States Bicentennial Celebrations. You probably remember that much from the "about the author" section of Zippy. And much like Mark Cohen, he was raised in the Dallas suburb of Plano – yeah, THAT Plano. He went to college at the University of North Texas. He spent a few years working as a boring consultant. And as of this printing, he's currently pursuing a Juris Doctorate at Texas A&M University School of Law. He's also a licensed Private Investigator in the state of Texas.

Since releasing the first print of Zippy, he's moved back to Plano. He still excels at knowing all kinds of useless facts. He is still part of a rock band called Arkei, and plans to release all 12 of Arkei's albums to Amazon within the next year or so.

And then one day, when he's forgotten how much intense work it is to write a novel, he'll sit down and hammer out M-Gang Chronicles: Book 3.